Office

Sumit Aggarwal is the author of *Office Shocks – A Novel* along with some other published, self published (on blog), unpublished and to be published works. He is currently working on his next book. He lives somewhere in Delhi and works at two full time positions – one at some office and the other out of his study or sometimes cafés.

Office Shocks

a novel

Sumit Aggarwal

RUPA

Copyright © Sumit Kumar Aggarwal 2011

First Published 2011
Second Impression 2012

Published by
Rupa Publications India Pvt. Ltd.
7/16, Ansari Road, Daryaganj,
New Delhi 110 002

Sales Centres:
Allahabad Bengaluru Chennai
Hyderabad Jaipur Kathmandu
Kolkata Mumbai

All rights reserved.
No part of this publication may be reproduced, stored in a
retrieval system, or transmitted, in any form or by any means,
electronic, mechanical, photocopying, recording or otherwise,
without the prior permission of the publishers.

Sumit Kumar Aggarwal asserts the moral right to be
identified as the author of this work.

Typeset in Warnock by
Mindways Design
1410 Chiranjiv Tower
43 Nehru Place
New Delhi 110 019

Printed in India by
Shree Maitrey Printech Pvt. Ltd.
A-84, Sector-2, Noida

This is for everyone dear to me; family & friends

Contents

Author's Note   ix
Office Memo   xi

The First Shock   1
   10.15 a.m.

The New Meat Meets Kitchen   6
   11.35 a.m.

The Mind Rebels at Stagnation   14
   12.15 p.m.

The Tiffin Terror   21
   1.30 p.m.

The Real Induction   29
   3.15 p.m.

The Office Devils   34
   4 p.m.

Nice Guys Work Overtime 4.25 p.m.	45
Ride to Nowhere 5.45 p.m.	55
Rendezvous with the Ravishing Rapier 6 p.m.	59
Highway to Hell 6.45 p.m.	71
A Hard Day's Night 7 p.m.	74
Damsel in Distress 8 p.m.	82
In Two Shakes of a Lamb's Tale 8.37 p.m.	87
Still, Let's Call it a Day! 9.01 p.m.	93
Epilogue Off-site Shocks	95

Author's Note

Dear Colleagues,

Office Shocks is a seriously humour-rich literary effort towards comic relief for office goers, office cynics and to-be office goers alike.

The refreshing dive into the deep end of the protagonist's head will purge you of the cardinal sin of not enjoying office thoroughly; for office is nothing more than a place where extreme contradictions and contradictory extremes exist; not to mention the opposing poles and polar bears (basically some seniors with a looming appetite for juniors and new-joiners).

Your copy of *Office Shocks* will keep you thoroughly entertained through any office journey. As an after effect of reading it; you might find yourself smiling, laughing and giggling throughout your office life during office hours.

Offices have a universality which is perhaps unparalleled. The peculiar and common character traits of people in office and people in general remain eerily consistent across office spaces, whether it be in the real world, your imagination or your dizzy daydreams!

However, this novel is a work of fiction. All characters, places and instances that appear in this work are fictitious. Any resemblance to a real instance, place and persons, living or dead, is purely coincidental.

I hope you enjoy the book.

If you do, please put in your comments on www.facebook.com/officeshocks. Also check out the page for some hilarious *Office Shocks* inspired content.

Wishing you happiness, increments and bonuses.

Warm Regards,
Sumit Aggarwal

Thanks to all the office folk and those who will join them and a special thanks to my five first days at four offices.

Regards,
Sumit
Office Shocks

Office Memo

To: God; friends; Rashmi Menon, Arjun Pereira, Rupa Publications; Office folk; Offices
Cc: Aniket
From: Sumit
Date: Some day in September 2010

Subject: ACKNOWLEDGEMENTS

Dear Colleagues,
   PFA, my good wishes for you all.
   This is to thank all of you who made this book possible.
   Thank you, God.
   Thank you, friends for your feedback and support.
   Thank you, Rashmi for being a great friend and critic.
   Thank you, Arjun for the meticulous edit work.
   Thank you, Rupa Publications.

Roses were certainly not my thing. I was glad they weren't there. Still, the bouquet looked nice and fresh. It had countless of those expensive and pompous flowers that have no fragrance; but are beheld as beautiful because everybody knows how much money has been paid for them.

⌒

The First Shock

10.15 a.m.

'WELCOME TO CAIRN & COMPANY, DEAR BOY,' SAID THE SENIOR manager of the department handing over the bouquet to me.

'Everyone!' he addressed his team aloud, 'This is Aniket and he is joining our team from today as a Junior Associate.' It was one of those exceedingly annoying designations that never told you what your exact role would be, not undermining the presence of the word 'junior', which was equally demeaning.

Everybody clapped and beamed. Was this for real? First, the pickup in the morning in a Toyota and now, this treatment! It felt as if it was a prank, or a dream, or a figment of imagination, but whatever it was, it was surreal.

Probably, the bouquet was symbolic, like a signal for the brickbats that were to follow. And the clapping was the beginning and would soon turn into these very people laughing, jeering and slapping the desk on some amateur mistake.

'Suresh will show you around and introduce you to everyone individually,' said the boss, pointing towards a pig-like guy wearing the strongest perfume known to mankind. He had a paunch and the white shirt he wore did nothing to hide it. And then, of course, there was that tie. The tie which is the symbol of the 'short leash' that the corporate world keeps on was right there. It was the clichéd dark blue and very ugly, more so because it bulged up front with the protruding paunch, snake like. And as if this was not enough, to add misery to ugliness, he had a smile on his face and the message it conveyed was, 'I am not ashamed. I know what you are thinking about me and I am glad that I developed a thick skin to counter such a stare.'

I was taken, then, escorted to every cubicle like a show dog that is made to do a round of the amphitheatre before the grand finale, the slick trick. After innumerable handshakes (some of them eager enough to crush my hand to pulp), we-know-all smiles and 'Welcome to Cairn & Company' lines in some seriously creepy and impersonal, robotic accents, I was shown my desk.

Luckily, it was the one near the window. Since, the office was on the eighth floor, the view was insanely nice. A workplace with a view of the city skyline is an office luxury, a consolation of sorts. I mentally punched the air jubilantly, and sat on the fat chair.

'This is for you. A laptop will be assigned to you in about a day or two. Get a feel of the place, roam around, chat to people and feel free.' Mr Suresh had obviously been busy before his senior, my boss, barged in on his business, disrupted his flow of thoughts and told him to introduce me to some people without his consent or wish. It was evident in the way he slid into his seat and stared at his computer screen with a hungry smile, hands in an awkward position, ready to start typing midair. Perhaps, some e-mail needed an urgent reply.

As for me, there was no laptop and consequently, no work. I slid my fingers over the desk. The surface was cold and smooth – the two adjectives valued in this jungle. A white steel board that could be used to write on with a marker or post a reminder on with a magnet, hung by one side of the cubicle. It would not be a stretch to imagine how valuable the quality of being 'magnetically sticky' would be.

My desk was at some sort of an invisible but prominent border with the other department. Across the border, I could see girls clad in *salwar kameezes*, and guys in half-sleeve shirts with ties (which just looked dumb). They were chit-chatting informally. It clarified the conspicuousness of the intangible border, but confused my sense of inter-departmental harmony. Just because my department faces the client once in a blue moon, whenever there is a goof-up by any of the executives or associates or a need for speed on any query, we have to wear a full-sleeve shirt and a tie. What kind of justice is that?

Screwing the justice then, my attention was raptly taken by the scruff by a fair maiden who had just risen from her throne to show her face. The sight could have given the inspiration to Shakespearean descriptions of someone in love or a description of the first sight of a beloved, a run for its money. She was talking to a guy who looked like her boss and who also looked, I hoped, married with a wife in the same department and two kids growing up to serve this same department in this company so that they could spy over him to keep him away from ever even considering something indecent with her mesmerising prettiness.

Crap! My reflexes were not timed to perfection and certainly not timed to hide my forehead and eyes in time as I lowered my gaze and shifted focus in a jiffy. Her eyes had noticed mine checking her out; or maybe, drinking her beauty in; or maybe, just floating only inches away from her, right in the office, inviting the wrath of the 'Social Sensitivity' clauses that would probably serve as a source of some good gossip for the HR department.

Whether she had noticed me or not, I could make out her forehead moving towards the archives room. She strode off to something important which spelled my inability to set eyes on her again in the morning.

'Hi!' piped a squeaky voice from the desk next to mine. I immediately turned my chair to look at the face and dimensions of a girl who befitted the profile of that 'squeaky voice'. She had a pale, freckled face with a mellow red glow on her cheeks, big black eyes, a short snout, a low forehead and very curly jet black hair that absorbed the light around. The reason that I could describe her face with such precision was the proximity of her face to mine, or perhaps it was the situation itself that made her face appear zoomed-in in front of my eyes. This also meant that my vision was stuck with her face in it and that I could not escape, not even to that happy place in my head, for the next few minutes that she would take to complete the normative obligations for an introduction and some general chitchat.

'Hi, I am Shivangi,' she squeaked and shot out her hand at me simultaneously. My quick reflexes allowed me to save my eye from her razor-sharp nails. I shook her hand nonetheless.

'Hi, I am Aniket.' That was all I could say.

The First Shock | 5

'So ... you are the new meat here. Cool! These guys are going to have their fun with you!' She said this with such a convincing and perfectly spooky chuckle that the spook landed home. I found myself suppressing a chill.

'Wh – what kind of fun?'

'Oh!' She looked at my face and started laughing. Between the laughs, she managed to say, 'No ... nothing like 'that' ... no ragging ... just that they are going to take your case, make you run here and there ... just wash their so-called ... oldness in the organisation ... on you ... just to show how much of smart alecs they really are.'

I grinned sheepishly. 'For a moment there, I was getting all sorts of weird ideas.'

'Sorry, if I scared you. But that was how I got my fun off you.' She smiled.

'Point taken!' I bowed a little thinking that she could be one of those cool people to be in the good books of.

We continued to chat for about one whole hour. She would check her Outlook inbox now and then and continue her conversation with me. But then, nothing could prepare me for what happened next. I immediately regretted having a good sense of wit.

'Hey, you should really get to work now with all those mails flashing on your screen. They might let off the new guy, but you might just get yourself a one-way ticket out of this place.'

There was a dirty, murky, dead silence between us. She kept looking blankly into my eyes. I got scared again. And it was not without reason. Tears started welling up in her eyes.

The New Meat Meets Kitchen

11.35 a.m.

'THEY ALREADY TOLD YOU THAT I HAVE BEEN GIVEN ... THE ... THE pink slip! These morons are horrible gossiping assholes!'

'Hey ... hey ... I was just kidding. I didn't know a thing ... I have just been showed around the place ...' 'Showed around!' Considering the parade I had gone through, that was a valid grammatical error.

I had already opened her emotional floodgates. I left my seat hurriedly as I let her uncontrollable sobs fall on my deaf ears and on some observant but ignorant conniving eyes (the neighbours in the next cubicle had suddenly lost interest in their con-call).

That experience was so horrible that a loo break was right in order. The first day's gaiety had been totally ruined and I thought that it could not get worse. Wrong again.

I made my way to the washroom. My instinct had told me to hold it in and go back to the seat. But, my sad luck coaxed me to go in, meet Suresh who liked to stand at the very next 'reliever' (no dividers here, long live western standards) and blabber, while you peed or at least pretended to pee or just hoped that the weirdo got it over with quick enough for you to attend to the piss in peace. The insane scumbag was in no hurry.

I was forced to move out and go to the washbasin. And immediately, Suresh moved too. What perfect timing!

Nonetheless I pretended to be busily checking something on my face. As the cliché goes, corporate life changes you. My attempt was to figure out the effects of a two hour exposure to its radiation.

'Hey, did you check out Purnima distributing sweets?' he continued.

The guy was a pervert to say the least. What would he get from 'checking out' a girl while she was sharing sweets to celebrate some happy event? I had to resort to the literal translation against what the nincompoop meant.

'Yes.'

'Did you eat some?'

No, I took it and threw it back at her face, abusing her like a lunatic.

'Of course, the sweets were nice.' I replied as innocently as possible. 'She told me she had gotten engaged.'

Suresh just laughed heartily and said, 'As if *that* is any cause to celebrate or share sweets. I mean, is it fair that the office eye candy is getting formally hooked?'

I did not understand why he could not just hear himself saying the most stupid thing; as if you had grand plans of going beyond ogling at her figure.

I just smiled along wryly and let the matter go. It would not fit my agenda to knock at his vacant temple.

He just rinsed his hands, shook off excess water wildly in the washbasin and reached out with one of those half-wet, half-germy hands towards me. I dodged his hand in time to see that he was actually reaching out for the paper napkin dispenser on the wall next to where I had been standing.

'Well, catch you later.' He walked out the door after having scored a 'friendly joke point' on the weird joke about the 'office eye candy', which was a sacrosanct teaching from his male-bonding finishing school lessons.

'Yeah, bye!'

I went to the urinal once again, and this time was able to relieve myself. While at it, the washroom was unrealistically quiet, and I could hear about every plumbing error in the vicinity. Somewhere, a pipe was dripping onto an already full pool of water that had formed due to the uneven placement of floor tiles. Something was scurrying in the AC duct overhead. Some girly whispers and giggles were faintly bouncing on my eardrums. I went to the washbasin and washed my hands. The giggles grew clearer and I could make out a few women talking.

The women's washroom was wall-to-wall with the men's washroom. Even if someone did not have a natural inclination towards eavesdropping, they would have felt their gut whispering that the conversation was somehow related to them. I followed my instinct and found the source of the sound leak. It was the ventilator outlet next to the washbasin and funnily enough, it was at a put-an-ear-to-it height.

Someone was saying, 'Yeah, and did you notice his perfectly formed ass?' More laughter ensued. 'I wonder what he would look like without those godforsaken formals...' 'You mean in casuals...' 'No, no ... just without formals!' More of roaring, uncontrollable and hysterical laughter. Then, there was the sound of the door opening.

'Girls, you are too loud. What are you hee-hawing about?'

'The new meat of course ... what else?'

I could not suppress a smile. I was the topic of discussion among the women of this cadre, and to top it all, them discussing a new joiner's physiology was unprecedented. Whatever next!

I excused myself from the nonsense out of the washroom and made my way back to my desk, mouthing certain expletives and swearing loudly in my head.

I noticed five minutes later that my neighbour was gone. The laptop had been left behind, abandoned and the chair was now tucked under the desk where it lay aimlessly, papers strewn all over. The drawers were partly open, mostly emptied of her stuff. She had cleared out long before her exit time. The heartless corporate culture had got to her.

As I was thinking about her plight, I found my boss clearing his throat loudly. He was standing next to my desk.

'Phone *utha liya kar*, yaar,' he said, sounding annoyed.

Yaar? Yaar? This last bencher in or probably someone who entirely skipped 'office etiquette one-o-one' had started getting on my nerves!

'It did not ring, Sir.'

'Well, it would have if you connect the wire to the socket,' said the boss curtly. Clearly, even coincidental insubordination was not under his list of pardonable actions.

He handed me a few papers.

'Get them scanned from the scanner on the fifth floor. You can take the login and ID of Shivangi.'

He handed me a yellow sticky note with an ID and password scribbled on it.

'Log in using this and send the scans through her mailbox. Understand?'

Yes, you dumb rascal. Anyone can understand such basic stuff. And, I can even tell you that this is going to take me forty-five minutes just to get the papers scanned from your ancient office scanner.

'Yes. Consider it done.' I smiled politely.

He left my desk singing a casual 'thanks' and headed for the fifth floor.

While waiting in the lobby for the lift to arrive, I caught a glimpse of something that looked like that royal beauty from the department across my cubicle. She had just turned the corner to enter the lobby area. She was walking towards where I was while I walked away from her, my back turned towards her. This should put me up as the 'non-interested, harmless, non-glaring type'.

Now as I turned to walk up the lobby again, I had the perfect excuse to not glare but sneak a peek at this scintillating, almost tantalising beauty and walk towards her on the pretext of walking by her.

As soon as I came close enough to exchange pleasantries with her, the melodious 'ting!' of the lift's bell sounded its arrival. So, there we were together in the lift, when we exchanged our first words and I felt a slight hope of her not having discovered me secretly leering and staring at her.

'Which floor?' I was standing near the control panel.

'Fifth floor, please.' My heart jumped with joy, did a few moon-walks, some break dance and calmed itself.

'Oh sure!' I replied as I pressed the round fat button that said 5.

'You joined today?' she asked to my delight. I would not have had a clue to start off that conversation.

'Oh yeah, how did you know?' Stupid question.

'You are taking a stack of important looking papers to the fifth floor for scans that usually consume a lifetime.' She smiled as she folded her hands loosely and in a very ladylike fashion.

'Yeah,' I smiled, 'First day first task is beyond my job description. I got the message. But how did you land up getting a trip to the scanner?'

'It's not for office work.' She smiled mischievously. Ting! Fifth floor had arrived.

She moved out first and I trailed behind, trying to keep up.

We entered the fifth floor as she touched her key card to the reader. The translucent glass gate opened to a corporate haven. Whatever department it was, it had the most elegantly dressed corporate folk anywhere. The guys had style and the girls on this floor exalted their appealing demeanour and seemingly appealing disposition in a chic manner. Busily chatting away on the phone or typing away on the laptop or discussing some important issue fervently with a colleague made them look like Greek goddesses dressed in trousers.

She must have looked back and noticed me with my mouth agape with reverence. 'This is where all the consultants sit.' I wasn't surprised.

Meanwhile, her royal prettiness led me to a corner in the office. I spotted an old monitor perched at the edge of the table with a scanner kept alongside. The state of the poor PC was obvious because scanning was the only function of that machine and it was not given as much respect as was endowed on other machines.

'Can I go first?' Now there are a few reasons that I could not have anticipated this, apart from her obvious mesmerising effect on me. However, the point is, she had been playing me right from the time she saw me holding a stack of papers and strolling in the library. Now, that was a bit too impressive and attractive considering it was actually still very annoying.

'Sure!' I said with little effort. Tip of the iceberg!

'Thanks.' She busied herself with the machine. Just when she put her document in, she got a call. The ringtone was default Nokia. I hated that.

'*Ahaan*! Okay. Alright. But ... is it really that urgent? Okay. I am on my way.' Her conversation somehow appeared more dramatic than it should have been. Instinct told me that. Then, the inevitable occurred.

'Hey, it is an awful thing to ask you to help me, but could you please send me this scan as soon as it is completed. You can use the login and ID that is currently on for your scans as well. Just do a save draft for me.' She was smiling. She was fluttering her eyebrows at me. She nodded lightly as she made the request. I nodded along.

You see, whenever a girl does her thingamajig magic, time stops. You cross over to another realm, the realm of affirmation. Everything around you is dawdling transition. The only sound you hear is that of the girl. The only thing you see is her face. And the only thing you are allowed to do in that realm is to nod!

'Thanks. That is very nice of you!'

'No problem.' Next time I would make you eat this piece of paper instead of scanning it for you, was the only thought I had. I wouldn't lie. I did imagine it too. It was an entertaining thought. I felt devilish.

'Just please remember to log off.' She wired a platonic wink and went off without another word.

I slumped in the chair next to the darned machine and habitually glanced at my watch.

I realised that she had left the paper she wanted scanned with me. I would have to take this paper to her desk to return it; like a minion on an errand.

The Mind Rebels at Stagnation

12.15 p.m.

'NO WONDER GIRLS MAKE FAR BETTER MANAGERS.' I SAID ALOUD.

Almost half of the day was just about getting over. Soon it would be lunch time. And till lunch I had all the scanning to enjoy.

Boring. Boring. Boring.

One by one, the scans took entire millenniums to complete. The age-old machine was taking away time from my life along with its last moments of practical use. I was impatiently tapping at the desk and humming an AR Rahman song. I was already through with checking my e-mail and facebooking, but considering that even using Internet Explorer slowed down the scanning, I had to get back to the tormenting ennui.

It is very unfair when humans design such situations for other humans. The cognitive dissonance combined with the neural activity that conceives associations is tingled beyond control and a fight starts in your brain. The brain locks and loads your five senses (six in case of dogs) into searching for ammunition in the environment to obliterate either of the conflicting associations. Then, welcome to the big fight!

In the red corner weighing in at five grams and fifteen pages, you have a totally inhumane task of scanning documents and in the blue corner weighing lesser than the common human and dressed three times more stylishly, you have the beautiful people of this heavenly floor. Ting! Ting! Round 1.

Ears hear a discussion of the latest book review in the latest revised issue of a cultural magazine. Blue wins!

Round 2!

A few consultants can be seen playing a scratch-and-win contest. And no, they are not scratching any card. They are too environmentally friendly to scratch papermade cards. They are consumedly scratching their misspelt 'lions'. Yes, ladies and gentlemen, this is the "scratch the crotch contest". Catch the highlights at the cubicle right opposite to the scanner where the divorced thirty-something sits. Red wins!

Round 3!

My nose takes whiff of a terrible, strong and effervescent aftershave lotion that is potent enough to choke flowers, sedate girlfriends to a coma or even turn off a whole factory of Viagra. Red wins!

Just when I thought that this is it, and the floor will always remind me of repulsive things, enter Tia!

Sometimes in life, you get a whiff of warm air encircling the exposed part of your formal collar-covered neck. The warmth spreads from the neck to the centre-left of your chest and then spreads to all of your body. And you can feel the last of the coolness on your fingertips as warmth takes over. The reasons for this phenomenon can be many. But the one that would be of cosmic significance in your life would be the entry of someone of the opposite sex in the periphery of your vision, in your zone of sensing, in the sensitivity threshold of your sniffing the sweetest scent, in the audible distance of the most rhythmic bass playing footsteps, etc. While this describes the input signals to the senses, the heart would be all calm, composed and would not even flutter. Numbness and warmth would restrict any body movement and that mouth that you wish was not gaping would not heed your self-respect's command.

Luckily, she was not looking at me during my span of recovery.

I looked pointedly at the monitor, very interested in the 'scanned status' and the slow and painful filling up of the status bar.

'Hey, how long will you take?' asked her sweet voice. The voice was somehow uncannily familiar.

I looked full at her face, peered into those large eyes and said, 'About five more minutes.' It was a lie. I wanted her to wait there for my five minutes and her fifteen at least.

We were now looking at each other as if trying to figure out something.

'Aniket!!??'

'Tia!!??'

That was the knockout punch. Blue wins!

'Oh man! It's been what ... seven years ... maybe more ...'

'Yeah ... it's been years ... but who's keeping count.' She winked her platonic yet aphrodisiac wink.

She was one of the hottest schoolmates to leave school right during the most romantically and emotionally challenged time in student life; breaking all the guys' and even a few girls' hearts. She was so hot that a few guys, reportedly, had to cry themselves to commit to assignments as a penance after she went to another school. I always knew that was on the cards – she had a way too cool a name and attitude to stick around too long at any place.

This bee's knees remembered my name and me. I felt cool.

'So how long have you been here?' I changed the document under the scanner as I struck up the 'catch up' conversation with the hot-cool girl next door from my school days.

'I have been here a few months. I am on the eighth floor.'

'Sounds cool. So how has it been so far?'

'It's been great. This is a decent place to work.'

'Hmm ... I'll find that out soon enough. Right now, I am really unable to contend with this donkey work my boss has assigned.' I was trying to sound as jovial as possible.

The reply that came was somewhat expected, but the serious expression with which it was said was uncannily unnerving. 'Trust me; there are worst bosses and assignments around.'

She said it in a serious dark whisper that got me all curious.

'What do you mean?' I tried to make the question sound casual and changed the last paper that she had to scan.

'Well, let's just say that in some dingy branches of the hierarchy, gender sensitisation and performance evaluation mean squat. I think you will stumble upon the different stories in circulation through the vine.' She winked at me at the end of the last sentence. I felt short of breath.

As she busied herself with the machine, I felt like it was a time as good as any to bow out; but not before I noticed some supposedly well-hidden dark circles that had that glaze which tears are supposed to leave.

'Okay, then. I'll see you around, Tia.'

'Take care, Aniket. You are a good guy.' She puzzled me with the 'good guy' remark. Whatever was that all about? Is it just me or do girls really abuse or overuse the expression 'good guy'? Whatever it is, it is very bothering. Because no guy is ever a good guy. They are bad or not bad.

Scanning is boring business. I decided it was time to prepare a 'new mail' and upload all the scans to be sent to ... err ... Girish. He had also written his e-mail ID on the yellow sticky note as if I couldn't check out the address list or as if Shivangi and he had never exchanged e-mail.

Before I could click on the 'new mail' button, I was sorely tempted by a curious looking HR e-mail.

Subject: Aid for Dr Rao's Family

I confess that my first glance at the screen registered the half-read 'auto-completed text as 'AIDS for Doctor Family.' The weird has a strange knack of affirming itself in the face of a duality. But then, even the correct mental analysis of the text sounded interesting.

Since when had these organisations started to pick out families of white-collared professionals to help them out?

I clicked on the mail.

'Dear All,
You are aware of the tragic demise of Dr Kailash Rao who was a top consultant with us at our Mumbai office.

We have made arrangements to provide support to his family beyond our words and condolences. The directors have unanimously decided to forward financial help to the respected employee's family.

Thanks,
Smriti Kapoor
HR Manager'

The e-mail was a piece of art.

It guaranteed absolute agreeableness and affinity. The illusion of concern was that smug son of a gun outlaw who manhandled his servants, the employees, but did not leave any incriminating visible scars. After all, who was it that the man was working for when he met his doom, at that late hour in the night?

The e-mail was a piece of art that also triggered off multifarious stimuli.

It could illicit a multitude of emotional reactions that ranged from poignant arousal to a wry smile merited by a worldly-wise realisation depending on the dominant characteristic of the beholder.

The scrooge would speculate about the money, the kind-hearted (non-existent) would not give it a second thought, a value-for-money seeker would do an innocent 'reply to all' stating his affirmation towards the noble act, the jealous miser would wonder how much the organisation had decided to give to the family and earnestly say that the guy wasn't the one who 'deserved' to die.

Dwelling on this issue and with all the scanning done, I made my way back to my cubicle. The office seemed strangely vacant. And a big clock was now noticeable near my cubicle that told me it was lunch time.

The Tiffin Terror

1.30 p.m.

My stomach grumbled loudly, scornfully and disrespectfully.

The growl of my stomach was almost a rebelling shout to the authority of anyone around who might have played a hand in keeping me away from lunch. It was lucky that no one was around.

Almost everyone in my department, rather on the floor, had left for lunch. It was the day to follow the herd to be able to secure lush pastures, lunch information and more importantly, lunch, if it was supposed to be scarce or eatable only while still hot. The HR executive had told me about the fifty bucks lunch plate. It consisted of a buffet of boiled vegetables that had been introduced only to a scent of spices accompanied by some bland hot breads that supply enough complex carbohydrates to keep you working through the painful post-lunch session.

The canteen smelled strongly of nothing. I went to the guy standing next to the counter with all the steam coming out of it.

'Veg or non-veg?'

'Veg' I replied. You never know what passes for non-veg with canteenwalas these days.

'Rs. 50.' I handed him the note and gestured for a plate. The food did not look very appetising, but I had already paid for it. Sometimes, people just don't understand that having paid for something does not mean that taking the risk to eat it is acceptable.

'There.' He pointed to a stack of plates at one corner of the counter.

I took the plate, selected the most harmless and least bland looking vegetables, and handpicked three breads from the topmost layer of fresh hot breads. There was pickle too; the kind of pickle one would want to avoid and the least of the reasons for aversion would be the way it looked; like a strange cold thick soup with curious looking dumplings. Most likely it had been left alone for the fear that it might actually bite someone.

Office folk were already busy with their maid-cooked food in their non-fancy *'dabbas'*. The only non-embarrassing lunch boxes were with very proud and pompous-looking bachelors and newly married people with their self-prepared or homemaker-prepared delicacies.

I spotted an empty seat at a table that seated some people from my department.

'May I join you guys?'

'Hey, sure ... sure.' They said this in unison. But then, as I sat, two of the senior males in the group sniggered.

I ignored it then. I got to know the mechanics of the 'what and why' of it five minutes later. That chair had been vacant for a reason.

The person next to whom I had taken that seat pushed one of his lunch box compartments towards me. His expression, 'Please, do try some of this great food.'

I took a spoonful gingerly, lest I would offend someone at a new place. I placed it inside my unsuspecting mouth.

It tasted awful. Even as I was recovering with another morsel of the bland canteen food, I saw him place a piece of sweet almond dessert in my plate.

Others were a source of great inspiration that moment. The way they signalled 'sticking to their own food' by telling him that they are better off finishing their own food lest their better halves turn on them when they went back home with a not-so-empty tiffin was commendable. Luckily, I found my saviour, the wonder woman. She was probably one of the women who had been discussing me in that washroom.

The rescue mission was covert, subtle and partly sexy. First, casual eye contact right after she noticed that I was looking at the piece of sweet. Second, a half smile combined with the left eyebrow rising up, posing a question, 'do you really want to eat that?' Third, her chin rose with the right eyebrow now pointing towards the sweet. Lastly, she shook her head telling me that I needn't eat it and then nodding slightly with her eyes closed to assure me that leaving the sad dessert alone was a normal phenomenon.

Then as I was about to get up, her eyebrows met the top of the bridge of her nose and gestured me to sit my butt back down and wait until the 'tiffin terror' had excused himself.

'Thanks.' I beamed at the knight-in-crisp-office attire.

Instinct told me to turn my head towards the canteen counter. Tia was there, buying a chocolate and heading towards the outside lobby.

'Hey. I'll catch you later.' I hurriedly kept the plate in the used-plate pile, rinsed my hands in the running tap in the washbasin next to the pile, put some sanitiser on the hands in anticipation of a handholding moment or something to that effect and walked hurriedly towards where she had gone.

I came out in the open to a large and open compound, with a walkway that visibly wreathed around the buildings. She was walking alone in the bright summer afternoon sun. It was not hot though. The cool wind had picked up.

I calculated that I would be able to catch up to her and strike a good conversation initiated by her discovery of me walking absent-mindedly besides her, apparently and authentically lost in some consuming thought. It would leave us with 3/4th of the track to treat and talk.

The plan worked like a charm.

'It seems like the first day has dazed you. You look so lost and thoughtful.' Her voice was silken, somewhat husky and dreamy. If I had not noticed blotches of dried tears on the lower semicircular hollow of her eyes, I would not have guessed that she was actually fighting back some pain and tears while talking to me. I was being used as a pleasant distraction. That sounded cool although tragic too, for her.

'Office is not exactly what I had imagined it to be.' I looked at her face hinting the sympathy on my disappointment. 'Oh! I mean to say that it has been all that and much … much more. Anyways, what is bothering you?'

My question had caught her off-guard. Girls have this long-standing belief that they have their crying minutes well covered by the quick-fix that consists of just dabbing handkerchief over the tears to dry them.

'Oh! Nothing at all. What makes you think that something is bothering me?'

'I usually pay heed to my intuition. I don't really know how it happens, but I can always tell if a person has some nagging problem in life.' It was as great a moment as any to highlight the enigmatic features of my being that includes clairvoyance among other things. Girls surely dig that. Only if they would realise that everybody, every single soul has some nagging trouble in their life.

'Hmm ... actually, even I connect on that front with my friends. Umm ... this work life is beginning to get to me. When I came here, it was so good. I felt like I belonged here. I found love here in the most unexpected way as I could have imagined. And then, now ... have seen such weird, unfair, things happen ... it has really rattled me.'

'I can't say that I am an expert on this place, but I agree; my first-ever neighbour on the eighth floor already left office. Rumour has it that she got a pink slip and just left in the morning itself too ashamed to stick around. It was very sad.'

Her eyebrows puckered as if bothered by that description. She seemed to fight a battle in her head between what was the right reply. A little shake of the head signalled a decision. She palmed her eyes; exhaled noisily and said something oblique with an effort to make it sound as an obvious follow up to the discussion. Common sympathy towards that girl's plight would become a device used by many guys on my floor as a conversation starter with the fifth floor divas.

'Oh! You should see what grand exits people get when they leave otherwise. You would think that the company could not be more of a humbug. But that is just a pleasant way of telling some not-considered-worthless employee that they are rich enough without him and he would really miss more of these grand lunch parties at top notch restaurants.'

The general behaviour towards their kind seemed appalling at first, but on second thought, it seemed fair treatment. Emotions at the workplace are for the weak.

'Wow! What hypocrites! And talking about exits, I heard about some Dr. Rao who passed away. It is weird that they allow people to work for the company beyond their retirement age.'

'Whoever told you that Dr. Rao was so old? He was forty-something and what everyone knows for a fact is that this brilliant guy with a PhD in Strategy was found dead in the morning in the Mumbai office. Doctors ascertained the exact time as 3 a.m. Probable cause was work stress. He was the famous workaholic in the organisation who never went beyond becoming a senior consultant.'

Hard work never hurt anyone? Yeah right, like a speeding maniacal mammoth of a 120-wheel Fighter Tank carrying truck it didn't! Whoever said this never lived beyond the early stages of globalisation, and definitely never lived in the developing nations that are sacrificing the present for a better future but getting lifestyle predicaments in return.

'That is so sad! Are all the people in this organisation worked up – so much so that the midnight oil drowns them? Some occupational hazard for the white-collared! This whole place is

Greek to me.' I found myself feeling very perturbed and it must have been evident on my face.

'Guess that wasn't a very tummy friendly detail for day one. But your reaction, dear. You will have to learn to modulate that if you are going to survive here. Learn to fake all emotions while you can, Aniket ...' I could not hear a single word after that. As soon as she took my name, I looked at her and got lost in just sizing up all the details of her, otherwise perfect, somewhat sad face. I could just blink, nod and voice a few 'of course' and 'hmms'. She was telling me something important about how one's life could be very grand if one has a sweetheart working in the same office. I was too enamoured by the contours of her face to pay heed to the content or to anything else.

I did not notice that we had walked right back to the elevator doors on the ground floor lobby, got in the lift and halted at the fifth floor, her floor.

'Bye Aniket. See you around.' That meant that we weren't friends yet. But the possibility of friendship made coming to office worth it, for every day.

The phone rang. It was my mother.

'Hi Mum.'

'Hi Ani, how has been the day so far? What time are you getting back today? Don't let them bully you into working till late ...'

'Please slow down, Mum. Today is the first day. I don't think they will risk giving me a lot of work. Should be back by 6-7 p.m.'

'Had lunch?'

'Ya, Mum. I need to rush now. Will call back in some time.'

I had to hang up. I would not want the people in the lift to listen to a parent-child talk. Why did they have to stand so close?

Mothers are so worried about their boys entering the big bad corporate world. Although, not without reason. Some of their generic advice works wonders when applied to situations at work. E.g. Cross the road after looking both sides translates to cross the people only after looking at who is on their side. Finish your lunch packet translates into do not trade your good food for bad-tasting food, etc.

The lift went to the 10th floor and I absent-mindedly got off. I recognised that I was on the wrong floor as the place, which should have the 'fire exit' staircase, had an inviting terrace. I got back in the lift to go to the eighth floor against my will and decided to come to the floor with a mug of coffee for the much-talked about 4 p.m. break of the corporate lore.

Very happy with having discovered a haven conducive of meditative, windy, king-of-world type of pleasures, I returned to my desk only to find bird dropping on my desk. The eagle boss's green dropping had a message asking me to come to a training session. '3 p.m. training session in the boardroom,' said the sticky note. I checked the time.

The Real Induction

3.15 p.m.

I should have been there, 10 minutes ago. I gulped hard and felt the pit of the stomach tighten.

I was asking directions to the boardroom like a foreign tourist lost within the labyrinthine walled city. I even spoke loudly and clearly in English as if that would help. It did help that this was an MNC. It was embarrassing and hilarious, but I could not spare even a second to laugh. I entered the room expecting angry smirks but was relieved to find that the room somewhat darkened and the screen showing slides was the only source of illumination.

I was lucky. The door to the room was facing the screen. Only the presenter could see me. He could have seen me if the projector was not throwing light at his face and the screen. The door did not squeak or creak. There was a vacant chair right in the corner next to the door.

I sat there and noticed a sheet of paper lying in front of the person sitting ahead of me. The Times New Roman Italics Font 14 heading said 'Attendance – Training session 03'. Stealthily, I slid the paper with my index finger towards me and signed it using the Parker parked in my jacket pocket. Easy does it.

The training session was about how the associates could use the new online database and what kind of data could help us. The presenter was explaining everything in so much detail as if we all were some kind of idiots. Well, at least he was not explaining the proper way to double-click the mouse or yawn at the screen, wipe the keyboard and mouse off drool although it may have been a session in increasing stamina against yawning. Maybe, he had covered that before I entered the torture chamber.

A glance around and I could make out different classes of training session attendees. Section 1 contained the sleep-fighters battling heavy eyelids that were ready to lay down arms owing to bombardment of boredom. Next in line were the attention-faker-zombies staring wide-eyed at the slides thinking about the shopping they have to do from the superstore in the evening. Third, were the give-a-heck-critics ardently listening to the presenter and trying to figure out a mistake in the slides. Lastly, the gifted outliers like me who undertake artistic pursuits of sketching something and scoring with the new-joiner females sitting close-by, who appreciate art and earning the brownie points with the boss who then notices you taking notes and considers you the new blue-eyed boy of his team.

Daydreaming about the good life for myself, being the boss's pet was also part of the dream world panacea. I was prompted to snap out of it as light flooded the room suddenly. There was applause. Even the Q and A round was over.

The boss stood up to address the team looking particularly gleeful. 'Team! Good news! But I don't want this spilling outside. We are going for an off-site!'

An off what? These desperate people would cheer anything that sounds like an off. There was enthusiastic applause and mild hooting.

' ... Next month ... ' followed more applause and sounds of approval.

' ... In Goa ... !' People went ecstatic. There must have been something shady with the canteen food. Why were these people excited about something that sounded like a picnic, not with family, but with each other, the people that repulsed them? It had to be just about the trip being company-financed.

'Nothing is confirmed yet, but off the record, this offsite is going to be in Goa. With this note, off to work, all of you!'

The team suddenly stood up and began filing out of the room, murmuring and chattering interestedly, and I, who could not wait to be out of the room (I had entered late), had to wait for others to depart. This was partly out of courtesy and partly due to the fact that I got nabbed behind the inward opening door and was sandwiched between the vacant chairs and the table. People had to go around the whole perimeter of the conference table to be able to exit the room.

I tried my best to follow suit and get out of the room unnoticed, but my boss was standing right in the middle of the room and he gestured me to wait while everyone else got out. He had been making stern eye contact with me during his little speech. I could sense something sinister.

As the room got vacated, the silence became eerie. My boss and I sat at the conference table facing each other.

His poker face did little to tell me whether these summons were for getting to the session late or for something else.

'Why are we not wearing a tie today, Aniket?' It was for something else. And something lame.

Why was he bringing it to my notice now, God?

'Well, I wasn't sure that it was mandatory and the HR did not mention the dress code.' Pleading innocence was the only palpable plausible ploy.

'Well, I was wearing a tie when I interviewed you. Wasn't I?'

How could anyone not remember that tie? It was a bad knot and the tie was too short. Well, the design and colour of the tie mimicked barf. I specifically remember that it gave me the picture of a large stocky hound with a short greasy leash. It had made me laugh and sick at the same instance. It was a very strong reason behind my confidence in the interview.

'That's true, but sir ...'

'You can do well to call me Girish. You are a smart boy, Aniket. Please try and catch up faster than this.' To call a man roughly twice my age with greying hair and a serious moustache-bearing face by his first name is a very potent source of mental disarray. I would do that eventually. But that wasn't the end of what he was explaining to me, bless his pre-maturely senile age.

While he was talking, my gaze drifted from the triangle of his face to the projector, to the black marker, to the stack of brochures, to the other chairs and I wondered what would inflict most pain if I threw it at this guy. In the end, I decided that a punch to the nose and a knee to his groin would be apt. And then....

'Alright,' I nodded in agreement, to whatever behavioural adjustments he had demanded.

We left the room in silence. He made his way to his desk, while I sneaked off to the lift. The 10th floor terrace was calling me. The cool breeze and fresh air was already playing with my senses, beckoning me. The lift gates opened and I stormed towards the glass doors beyond which lay the corporate salvation, but I stopped short. I had just noticed something like a coffee machine in the small room on the far side of the lobby. A hot cuppa joy with cool breeze and view of the horizon was the complete picture.

The Office Devils

4 p.m.

I POURED MYSELF A CAPPUCCINO, CONVERTED IT TO A LATTE and then stormed towards the terrace. The glass doors were translucent. I could not make out what exactly the black blimps visible through them were. Anyhow, I enthusiastically opened the door taking a sip from my coffee simultaneously. The experience was a far cry from my wildest imagination.

As I stepped forth, the bright sunlight blinded me to stop me from looking at the scene, the cognisance of which came as my nose took in a whiff of the freshly exhaled tobacco smoke, while my ears caught some expletives from a part of a heated or overly excited lecherous conversation. My tongue was burning with the extremely hot and bitter coffee, and now to top it all, I could feel some dust particles that flew into my face probably from some repair work that was happening on the upper terrace. With all the five senses taking a beating, the inevitable words let themselves lose from my mouth, 'O sweet God Almighty in Heaven!'

Five minutes to recover and five seconds into recovery, I saw the reality of the terrace haven.

There were little chimney zones all over the place with groupings of two to four employees, mostly male. Some females could be seen with their cuppa joy and some with their ciggies and some with both! The smokers occupied the downwind part of the terrace and the drinkers marked the up wind part. Acting out of modesty of the inability to smoke, I went to my rightful place, the upwind part of the terrace.

I felt rewarded for tee-totalling when I saw Tia there looking away into the horizon (whatever of it was visible past the other surrounding skyscrapers). A girl pondering over something in the late afternoon and gazing into nothingness, standing over a dramatic view of the city was too filmy. Nonetheless, I thought she could use some company. Of course, so could I.

I went over to her, next to the railing. From a distance, it looked awkward that she was not holding on to the railing while gazing into the horizon and was even standing a good few feet away. But up close, the reason came to light. The railing had multicoloured sticky notes stuck to it, posted there by the friendly neighbourhood pigeons and definitely, eagles. These birds had fondly taken to the corporate timepass with using the space where their fly zone should have been.

After the initial repulsion from the dirtiness of the place, I turned my face towards her.

'Hi.' She noticed that I had been standing there; that someone had been standing next to her.

'Hey. You are already up for the afternoon terrace-break, Aniket! Not bad.'

'Thanks. Well, I did not expect to see you up here either. I always imagined you to be mobbed by your fans and friends anywhere you went.'

She smiled. I was her fan too.

'You are unfailingly kind, Aniket.' (The sound of her sighing …) That will change.' Her smile was more pursed now, somewhat sympathetic.

'What has happened, Tia? Is everything okay at home?'

'No. Nothing like that. I am just a little rattled by the goings on in this place.'

'Like?'

'I don't wish to burden you with my thoughts, although, I am sorely tempted. You are a good listener and still pure of heart.' Where had that come from? Somebody had been watching too many movies from the romantic era. Nonetheless, it was a compliment and I was beginning to enjoy this. And again, even her sadness came across as a minor detail that I could overlook.

'Tell me, please. Maybe I can help.'

She laughed lightly. 'No one can help what has happened. One of my friends was asked to leave this place, my only retreat available a phone call away has been taken, the only one who understood me. I am just too messed up thinking about what I will do now. This is all I can tell you. Please don't badger me for more details.'

'Of course not.' The word *badger* was a little insulting. I wondered whom had she confused me with.

I saw the glint of a golden tear welling up in the corner of her left kajal-laden eye. 'See you later, Anee.' She left me with a strange mispronunciation of my nickname and a truckload of enigma. I hated that pronunciation of my nickname. It made me sound like a dumb fat kid ... a double 'e' in the name!

My afternoon could have been spent peacefully pondering over Tia and her memoirs, but I could see some of the guys I had been introduced to in the morning smoking away in one of the corners. They waved a hand and beckoned me to join them. I did, against my repulsion and screaming scepticism.

One of the guys was the embodiment of a lesser known corporate adage that told something about working to make both ends meet, through a rather endowed and bushy uni-brow. Uni-brow is perhaps a very indigenous symbol of illustriousness and entrepreneurship. In this case it was just a sign of non-Darwinian acquiescence and inexplicable neglect. His crispy mauve shirt and the cufflink-ed sleeves told another story of how, as you climb up the corporate ladder, your hands become thinner and the paunch becomes stauncher. His shirt was bursting at the seams, stretched and screaming. He had perhaps jumped a few steps on that ladder in aspiration alone. His corporate look would have been complete if the teeth weren't already chrome-yellow denoting experience of many a cigarette.

The other guy was lanky but must have been hitting the gym twice a week. He had rolled up the sleeves of his shirt to beat the heat or perhaps to attract sophisticated female colleagues, his hope in heaven that they would be drawn to his thick, and hippopotamus' neck-like arms! His only saving grace apart from the corporate uniform with the embroidered luxury totemic-tag was the pair of black sheet spectacles combined with a well-groomed French beard that gave him an air of abandoned intellectual pursuit i.e. He tried, and thought better to just leave it alone. Or maybe not! Who could tell!

My reading of them told me that these were the dynamic duo of the department; Jai and Dhir.

Jai twisted his head to the side, pouted his cheeks to the left and let out some smoke for what I thought was some well-rehearsed attitude show-off or perhaps just an attempt to break one's own neck. I later found out that this was the new polite exercise of not blowing smoke directly into other people's face. He grinned.

'Hey buddy. Welcome. So how is the first day going, dude?'

'Hi.' The other guy just raised an eyebrow in return. He was busy doing the smoke-twist neck-exhale routine. 'It has been a nice day. Today was all about introductions, I guess,' I replied. I didn't have any answer for his eyebrow's Parkinson's move though.

'Yeah, man. You are lucky. I remember my first day. I was made to work like a dog ... not complaining though. And what else? I hear you are from The Management Institute of India, dude. But then, what are you doing here buddy?'

'Well, what do you mean? This is a nice company. They hire from nice colleges, right?' I was not sure what these guys were getting at. I was perfectly happy thinking that I had joined a recruiter-of-choice as the 'careers' section in renowned newspapers proclaimed.

The dynamic duo sniggered. 'Well, you will find out soon enough. These guys just hire anyone. It's not like they are asking us for rocket science as deliverables.'

'I guess I will. Anyways, how did you get to know about my college?'

'Well, the HR Department forwards introductions of all new joiners to everyone. It's interesting.' Jai winked. I cringed.

That means that everyone knew by now that I like to paint landscapes on the weekend, courtesy the HR scumbags, courtesy my CV, courtesy my dumb friend's advice to put in art under 'profound interests'.

'Great. Anyways, how is work like here? What time do you normally get to leave for home?'

This time, the duo burst out into low cough-like guffaws.

'It is all donkey work, mate. You will find out soon enough, bro. Did HR tell you that the official working hours are 9 to 6, eh pal?' he used air quotes for the word 'official'. Dhir had decided to break his silence and come forth with something erudite.

Anyways, now I knew the secret of the prefix 'official'.

'7.30, if I am lucky, pal.'

'Never before 9 p.m. every day, dude. I get laid every night. Only positive for me is no work on weekends, buddy.'

'Really?' The only possible explanation was a mispronunciation and careless listening.

'Oh yeah, man. Every night. Every damn night I get late.' There it was. It was the word damn that may have helped improve the enunciation of the 't' in late.

'Well, I too have to do weekends sometimes, mate.'

They were lying. Or even if they were not, I pretended it was just their life that did not exist. Otherwise, every employee brings his own workload fate in the organisation. I was not going to ruin my first day pondering over the potentially problematic and the imaginary, life-sucking demon of some workload.

Luckily, I did not have to say anything to conclude or change the topic.

Are you up for beer and rock music tonight, bro?' Enunciation of his 'r' was already slurring with a potent reverie of alcohol consumption.

I did not deem it prudent to go drinking with these guys. It was nothing to do with silly notions about injurious nature of bad company. But, I ran the risk of being 'seen' with these two, and considering their *sui generis*, they would be hard to miss walking by whomsoever.

'No, thanks. I think I would just be happy to see the day through and go home.' Incorrect answer. 'X' gets the square. I found out later why it was the most inappropriate reply to that question.

'Yeah ... I understand, chief. Do you like your neighbour?'

'What?'

'Shivangi, dude. Don't act so innocent, man.'

'Well, I have only just met her. She has already left for the day, I think.'

They sniggered in unison again. It was irritating as hell like two pieces of nails scratching themselves against a chalkboard with unbridled gaiety.

'That hot thing has left for good, bro. She overstayed her welcome.' Bravo, another contribution by Dhir. He flicked the ash off the end of his ciggie as he made a statement that he had been practising for the last 30 seconds in his head.

'But, I don't get it. What did she do wrong?'

'Dude, it is about what she didn't do. She never did any sucking up and she sucked at her job anyways.'

I instinctively flapped my hand around my ear as if shooing away a buzzing fly as the two sniggered again on the very intelligent use of the word 'suck'. 'Don't worry. You will do fine. You seem like a comely chap.' Their reassurance sounded most sinister.

'Rumour has it that she was also seeing some dude in the office. Nobody knows who it was but Nihit ... the other team leader told me that her exit process was sped up due to those reasons.'

'That is crazy. You can't show people the door just because ... I mean that is so orthodox.' I did not realise how loud I was.

'Shh! bro. Keep it down. There is always an HR informant around.' Dhir, the *khufiya*, or the cagey one was at it again.

'What we do know is that she and her guy met at one of the off-sites with the help of one of our Japanese counterparts. It was her secondment. Ravi even swears he saw her making out with someone.'

'What the hell are these off-sites about? Just elaborate picnics?'

The Smug Sniggers had got an opportunity to perform again.

'Off-sites work like this. For ninety percent of the people, they are plain simple outings to get away from office and home, with office people, of course. Among the rest ten percent, half take the opportunity to get laid and half take the opportunity to get hooked up, man. Especially, studs like us.' He winked. Thank God it was only rhetoric.

'Oh, yeah! The HR training sessions and corporate trainings, company performance review are just for kicks, bro.'

The three of us went silent after completion of this information download and were staring in three different directions. I was thinking ... and these guys were probably enjoying the echo of their voice jumping around in the hollow of their skull.

After some time, Jai gestured to Dhir. And as if I did not know that they were being overtly covert right there, they pleaded a formal exit from the little meet.

They threw down their cigarettes and snubbed them under their polished leather shoe toes.

'Care for some?' asked Jai as he put a hand in his pocket and took out a fistful of those unbearably sweet breath mint candies. Sick. No thanks.

'Thanks, man.' I took one to throw over the balcony and check how far I could fling a thing of negligible weight.

'Anyways, we got to return to the work station. See you around.'

'Yeah, sure. See you around.' Not.

I realised that in the last half-an-hour or so I had actually amassed an inventory of unofficial designations, somewhat like the gods, but nothing even half as holy. I had been Buddy, Dude, Man, Chief, Mate, Bro, Pal, Chap and Stud. That, combined with Tia's Ani must make me eligible for a special guest appearance at the local Ramlila as Ravana's long lost white-collared brother who had ten names instead of ten heads or perhaps to revel in my own Dashavtar (ten incarnations). First name culture? In your face Girish!

Now, feeling glad that that was over, my spirit of adventure found me and urged me to explore the very inviting steel staircase leading to the upper terrace. There had been no sound of any construction work. I was curious about the dust particles that had flown into my face.

All this while, my coffee went conveniently cold; lukewarm enough now to 'officially' consider it as undrinkable and to just leave the cup at the parapet like I had witnessed other colleagues doing.

I was mentally counting the stairs. They wound around what seemed like the service elevator shaft. And the landing was at least

8 feet above. 1...2...3...4...5...6...7, I halted to listen more clearly to something like a 'commotion' going on. Something sinister was at work. I was in half a mind to get the floor security guard here. But, my Sherlock-inspired self pledged more investigation.

8...9...10.... I saw a few broken chairs on the staircase and up ahead was the final turn that would lead me to the landing.

The sound had hints of pain, frenzy, exhaustion, and hyperventilation. Excitement-filled prying stealth engulfed me as I peeped at the scene while hiding my body behind the elevator shaft.

My heart seemed torn between the cruel choice of terming the scene as a visual treat or as a display of animal lust.

The show was sponsored by the corporate park. A sophisticated and elegantly pedestrian name, some XYZ Corp Park was put up in bold letters carved in steel right about six feet above the place of 'action'. Then, to comprehensively appreciate the scene, I felt like breaking into one of those Animal Planet TV show presenters with a British/Australian accent.

'*Oyi*, what do we have here. Look closely. Be careful not to disturb them. Just zoom in for a better look. Yea. What we are looking at are humans. The curious little mammals that seem eager to discover the secret of aroma on each other's breath are actually performing what we biologists call foreplay. Look how the male grabs and gropes at the female but the female is not far behind. One way of looking at the corporate commandment – you lick mine and I lick yours. Fascinating.

'Now, to the layman, all this may be disgruntling but the act is beautiful. Look at them. Look at how they are together, in this moment. According to the religious heads of the aborigines of this region, right now these two are sharing not only the moment, they are sharing mind, body, soul and possibly, a very delicious chewing gum that both are eager to munch on. It is also a contest of sexual power between the two. And such is the magnanimity of nature; these creatures use everything in their natural habitat. We can see how they have put some broken office chairs to good use. The negligible essence of these chairs would be absolutely depleted by the time they are through with this call of nature or the erstwhile booty-call.'

Jeez, I cracked myself up. Paralysed with noise-cancellation hi-tech laughter, I strutted back down the staircase. The terrace was vacant.

Crap! I had spent almost forty-five minutes away from my desk. But still, watching two cautious analysts making out on the corporate park terrace with a perfect sense of timing, vision angles and sound muffling for minimising risk was worth it. Wily grin.

I made my way to my floor. I saw Jai waiting at my cubicle and turn around to look at me just as I walked into full view of the office.

Nice Guys Work Overtime

4.25 p.m.

'HEY. YOU DON'T HAVE ANY ASSIGNMENTS FOR TODAY RIGHT?'

I did not like the hunger in his words.

'Err. No'

'Great. Jeetji, he will go to the client for data collection.' He had caught me midway to my cubicle and now addressed the person next to whose cubicle we stood.

'What? But I ...'

'I have talked to Girish about this. He wants you to go and have a first time interaction with the client.' He thrust a folder in my hand and handed me a yellow sticky note with the address of the client's place.

'The folder has the questionnaire, a writing pad and a pen. The address is on the sticky note. It is in Okhla. The driver knows the place. The taxi is waiting for you downstairs.' He walked over to the lift as he said this, with me having to follow him in the line of duty. 'It's 5 p.m. I think you should be back in an hour.'

'But my bag and things are at my desk.'

'Don't worry. You have to come back in any case to drop off the data to Jeetji.'

Jeetji was too senior for anyone to call him Jeet.

I was shoved into the lift and the rascal winked as the doors closed.

Screwing the injustice for the second time in the day, I reached the reception. (Days later, I heard an interesting story from a colleague about a person who was heard swearing out to glory across three floors by senior managers waiting for the lift.)

I could not tell whether the receptionist was ugly or good looking. She wore a veil of makeup.

'Is the cab here for Girish's assignment?'

'Wait for five minutes.' She gestured me to wait seated at one of the large undemanding chairs.

Ten minutes into waiting, two girls barged in to the reception area.

'Hey, Nalini, do you have some aspirin by any chance?'

'No yaar. But, we can ask an office boy to get it.' Office boys were the highly revered minions who carried out the corporate devils' bidding.

'Okay. But, let me call Sundar. He might have one.'

'Sure. Use this phone.'

As she was making the call, I noticed that there was a lump on her belly. I had surely caught some weird joke about some 'belly' as the two women had come into earshot.

'So, it's been four months?' asked the receptionist.

'Yeah.' She smiled.

'Hey, what are you waiting for here?' Someone asked this rather loudly from the lobby, in Hindi. *'Kiska intezar ho raha hai?'*

Corporate male would not give up a chance to flirt with any girl. Engaged, married, pregnant, single, etc. If moves, can flirt.

The lady's reply came like a punch, 'the lift, d-uh.' The girls laughed condescendingly.

It was totally slick!

Also, because at that same moment, the girl said 'du-uh', the lift said, 'ting!' and the guy went in hurriedly.

I smiled, thoroughly enjoying the show. Ten more minutes went by. The receptionist second-guessed me with a shake of her head when I lifted mine to ask her the status.

More wait was ominous. I picked up the pink newspaper and busied myself.

There was a Toyota advertisement on the front page. The thought of reliving that pleasant car ride in the morning filled me up. I had begun to imagine myself sitting on the back seat and enjoying and not merely reading the newspaper.... The thought of Aniket, the manager in a chauffeur-driven car going to visit the client was engrossing.

'Hey! You are goin' to Okhla, right?' I came back with a jerk to the reception area to see someone standing next to me and beaming.

It was Sumarrya. He was an assistant manager in another team of my department. Well, it was my department now.

'Hi, Yup ... I am. You ...'

'I need a lift till Mehrauli. I ended my work early today and have to get back to my four-year-old who is creating havoc at home.'

I was amazed, almost taken aback at his clear, confident voice. His voice combined with his very common face, was by the corporate contrast, immensely comforting. His smile had a very fatherly warmth, and his common brown eyes looked trustworthy.

'So am I allowed?' His humble rhetoric was scintillating. This dude was seriously out of place, time, era, country, age, etc.

'Oh! Of course. Of course.' I felt dumb.

He took a chair across mine.

'So you are the new Don Quixote.' I never expected anyone in the office to even know that such a combination of words and alphabets existed. I smiled.

'I must confess that I did make out the corporate to be grander ... no not grander ... but much more ... than it has portrayed itself in the day so far.'

'Well ... in the words of Randy Bachman ... you ain't seen nothin' yet.' That was too geeky. Even for this anomaly of a corporate half-honcho.

'Really?'

'I am not sure. But, who cares. It is the thought that matters.' He did not wait for a reply. 'Nalini!' He shouted authoritatively. She picked up the phone and did her thingamajig.

'The cab is here. Please proceed.' He went to the receptionist's desk and took a sticky note from her and came back.

'Let's go.' His face was still doing the Buddha act.

We stepped out together. I stared at the sky, as usual. The sunlight was not blinding, for there was a cover of bright glowing clouds that seemed to move with the cool wind that was trying its best not to uproot trees with even the most tightly packed branches and thick endowment of leaves. After a recon of the weather, my eyes started the search for the cab. It was nowhere in sight.

Not being able to find the car, I turned towards Sumarrya and presto! I could not spot him either.

'Oyi! Aniket!' He was shouting from my blind spot. The spot being denoted as 'blind' because I had seen an Indica parked there. Surely, that was not supposed to be the cab.

But, he was still walking towards that car. I followed. As we reached the cab, he smiled.

'You were expecting the Toyota. We have all been down that road. Don't be embarrassed. You will soon come to terms with what the admin department in this place, or rather any place, is all about. If you are someone from any other department, you are on their torture hit list.' People who know everything are so damn irritating.

I sat in the ramshackle of a cab. We sat on the back seat with his laptop and bag occupying the space in the middle. Someone standing outside could describe it as cosy but it was definitely not comfortable. In addition, I swear that someone would be whimpering and whining in pain after voicing out any such description. I would beat that rascal black and blue.

I had not noticed the driver. He had already taken his place at the driver's seat. The driver was by far the most ancient person I had ever seen. His *beedi* was joyously going flame red at the tip each time he took a puff. As and when he looked at the sahibs take their seats, he threw out the beedi and asked for the destination.

'Go to Mehrauli and take a right for Okhla. After that, he will give you further instructions.' His Hindi was also meticulous.

'Ji Sahib,' replied the ancient driver. He started the engine and the car lurched on sputtering and stuttering ahead.

'Hey, can you turn on the AC please?' It was a few degrees too high in the car and also stuffy. The car reeked of tobacco and felt a little damp.

'Nahi Sahib. It doesn't work.'

'You really feel like killing Girish now, don't you?'

'Well, I was thinking of taking the matter up with him. Jai was supposed to be on this job and not me on the first day.'

'C'mon yaar. I didn't expect you to be so short-sighted. You want to start squeaking from day one?'

'Squeaking?'

'The wheel that squeaks gets oiled, Aniket. If you squeak too much, your boss will just keep on piling donkey work at you till you get wasted going over it again and again and just quit, either squeaking or the job.'

'Then what do you think is the best tact?'

'Become the support system of the team. Make them get used to your efficiency. Get the bargaining chips. And that certainly doesn't mean that your social life has to come to an end. Do you have what it takes to be a weasel?'

'A what?' The driver coughed loudly. It did not mean that he knew what a weasel was.

'A weasel. Can you delegate to people on the same wrung of hierarchy; can you shift responsibility of poor outcomes; can you get out of late evening editions of the boss's love for your life; can you still be the best employee of the department and can you, in short, seamlessly weave other people together?'

Err ... hmm ... and a house-fly's buzz was all that was running through my brain. Corporate was going to be heavier than anything

I had imagined; as if already, the eye-opening, madness-gauging events hadn't taken place.

'Seriously, Aniket. You should start reading more. Do you know who Scott Adams is?'

'Oh! Dilbert!' He had been taking my Mickey with the whole Weasel business. The smart-alec had had five minutes of fun at my expense.

'That Jai did a perfect execution of Dilbert. But, do you know why he targeted you? Why were you the most alluring and naive catch of the day?'

That really got me thinking.

'It is just my first day. I hardly know the person. I think it was instruction from the boss only.'

'My naive Edmond. This goes beyond some simple conspiracy. Is there anything you might have said to him or offended him or anything?'

I was still thinking. My eyes were on their usual thinking mode, searching and scanning the space around me wildly to locate some object of mental association with the event that had caused Jai to bestow such niceties.

In an answer to my question, the clouds parted in the instant we came out to a clear open road with no tree cover on the side to hinder the sun as its rays fell on this man's engagement ring bursting into clear sparkles flashing into my probing gaze. There was a mental flashback. The sparkle of this ring had dazed me before.

I felt light, weightless as I realised the mind-boggling, rattling truth. The hand that was groping that female behind on the upper terrace of the tenth floor balcony had a ring with an unmistakably similar shine.

I looked at the face of this infidel, two-timing, polygamist. He was staring out the window at the metro line construction, waiting for my reply. And then my thought shifted to the conversation with Jai on the roof.

The clouds were back and this time, lightening struck them.

Of course! Declining the offer to go for drinks that evening had landed me a ticket to Okhla. I did not have any plans that evening and telling the truth in office had its consequences.

'Oh! The devils, the vile, cruel rascals.' There was something about this life that made people talk like people from books belonging to a bygone era.

I felt sick of two things at that time, one being the guy sitting next to me, the knowledgeable, geeky, extra-marital affair propagating, classic literature quoting, obscure music composer quoting, 'freaky freak' and the second being the 'out-to-eat-you' nature of people in the world of corporate offices.

'Yes. Now you know. Be careful the next time.' I couldn't stand this guy having an upper hand in a conversation with me. But then, he was a wisecrack and I could do with some advice. So I asked him, 'What should have been done then?'

'Always talk about some plans you have for the evening that you can crib about not having been able to attend when you stay till late in office and when you come to office the next morning.' He was really beginning to make me feel sick. On second thoughts, it was the stuffy back seat of the broken-AC Indica running amok in the Delhi traffic that was really making me queasy.

'Here, have a chocolate.' He was smiling cheerfully while he offered the chocolates kept on his open palm.

'Err ...' Was I supposed to take chocolates from a 'strange' creepy guy?

'Oh! Of course, you don't know about the chocolates. They were distributed before your training session, courtesy our boss. He returned from Switzerland yesterday.'

'Hmm ...' So, that is what these top brass people do. They bless foreign nations by gracing their tourist spots and bringing back chocolates.

'We get peanuts in return for the job and he goes on luxury holidays.' I was a little angry at the disparity.

He started laughing at my innocent statement.

'The writing is on the wrapper! Check it out.'

The chocolate was peanut-flavoured.

Between the guffaws, he managed to say, 'He always gets the peanut-flavoured or peanut chocolates wherever he goes. Have it, yaar. Peanuts are healthy.' He winked at me. I gingerly took the chocolate, a little flushed to act otherwise. I pocketed it later when sufficient time had passed to negate any perceived rudeness on not having eaten the chocolate there and then.

Finally, we reached the Mehrauli bus stop.

'I will give you one last unsolicited advice.' He was not going to let anything go even as he was getting out. 'Don't judge people by what you witness them doing. Nothing is personal.' He winked at me and left. Insult to injury. Did he know that I was a witness to this white-collared porn star's award-winning performance?

I was more in favour of calling it a coincidence, but I surely felt unnerved by this guy's self-assuredness. Was this the new meaning of success? To have a well-paying job, a kid to raise at home, probably a housewife taking care of his chores, a female to spend leisure time with in office, getting time to read literature, office humour and loads of crap?

Maybe, I would be somewhat friendly with this freak-show in order to extract (copy and paste) a few tricks of the trade pursuant to my strategic relief. It was plain sad that wisdom could be found at such unlikely places.

I did not notice that the car had not moved an inch for about ten minutes now. The traffic jam was mind-boggling. Delhi is the shopper's paradise and shopper's driver's purgatory.

Finally, after overtaking a few cars by changing lanes in a strategic game of signalling the intent to indent the neighbour's car, the wise ancient driver drove the fearless and feared, dilapidated Indica (that looked like a thug with scars on his face denoting affinity towards violence) to the edge of the traffic stop line.

By the next five minutes, we had taken a right turn on the road to Okhla, the filthy destination of all industrial pilgrims and the Goddess of wealth-praying priests in the national capital. It had minarets and chimneys shooting the clouds with dust and soot, belching charcoal and exhaling smog. These minarets were a part of fat constipated factories that expelled dirt in all forms on the roads, choking the industrial waste drainage system. The industrial waste drainage was a sham anyway – a few trenches dug on the roadside that absorbed the waste and waited for the rain and sun to get diluted and diffused into the atmosphere. The description now adding to my sickness, seemed incomplete. I had missed a vital detail.

Ride to Nowhere

5:45 p.m.

I STILL HAD FIFTEEN MINUTES TO REACH THAT DREADED PLACE. I opened the folder I had been given. It is only professional to have read about the person one has to meet.

I took out the four pieces of paper stapled together by the top-left corner.

Page 1 described the client. Page 2, 3 and 4 of the document contained parts of the structured questionnaire.

Against my nature, I consoled and coaxed myself into thinking that this would be a good experience to meet a CEO, take an interview and experience something new in the process. This consolation was my only hope.

The description of the client was as follows:

Organisation: Svelte Textile Exports Ltd.

Owner: Nisha Talwar

Business: 100% export-oriented manufacturing order processing unit

Query: Business Development, client acquisition
Address: ....
And so on ...

Nisha Talwar – the name sounded spiky. There was an edge to it. A female running a manufacturing unit of garments in Okhla sounded a little too sexy. Although, when I tried pronouncing her name, 'Talwar' made her sound old, scrawny, wrinkled and shrewd but only because of the association of the word with some age-old sword, now rusted and preserved in a museum, but used by some mythological hero in some epic battle hundreds of years ago. I hoped that it was not so. I had an instinct that I was about to meet a unique, definitely not unattractive, person. Therefore, there was certainly something to look forward to with this meet.

As my thoughts began to settle down, the universe conspired again to quite literally, unsettle them. A nerve-racking, vertebrae-vibrating, thunderbolt of a pothole rattled me to my intestines so much that digesting an ingested rock would have seemed to be child's play.

We had entered the Okhla Industrial Estate. It should have been re-christened 'what the hell' industrial waste.

There was no recovery or respite. Another pothole saw my head bumping the tall ceiling of the Indica. It was then that I realised that the seat belts are all a conspiracy. These drivers are safe from many such haemorrhaging contours crafted on Delhi roads because of the seat belt, which the companies fail to provide on the back seat. Even, if they do provide it to the taxi-operators, they sell it off as a spare or ask for a cash discount and removal of the passenger safety belt.

The only positive ray of hope out of all this was that at least I was not performing the stunt of drinking or holding a brimming and boiling hot cup of coffee at that time.

I was definitely on the verge of barfing in the car with the entire universe harrowing my senses. The non-AC car's open window brought with it puffs of horrible smelling fumes that built an image of dead and decaying organic substances in my head. The constant 'cradle for the wrestler's baby' approach as resultant from the harmony between the car and the road was twisting the food in my stomach that was awaiting digestion.

The only thought that kept me from throwing up inside the car was that of going back to office in a cab that had a terrible stench in addition to the perverse conditions that were already tormenting me.

At length, twisting and weaving through many twists and turns, the car made its way through Okhla and we reached the destination.

I got off the rickety petrol rickshaw of a car and stretched my limbs from fingers to toes. I looked at the grey, shabby and dirty factory-like building, compared it to the image of my new office space and felt obscenely haughty.

I told the driver to turn the car around and keep it parked nearby so that it was possible for me to come out and leave ASAP.

'Turn it around, bring it back and keep the engine running. I will be back in five minutes.' Without any particular reason, I had made it sound as if I was going to rob a bank. Interesting analogy ... consultant ... robber.

'You might take some time in there, sahib. Mind if I go get my lunch? I haven't had anything to eat,' replied the driver who was in no mood to rob any bank.

'Fine. *Theek hai*.'

I stepped inside from the front gate, which was open. A security guard appeared from nowhere and asked in a very suspicious manner, '*Kisse milna hai?*' – but it sounded more like 'What are you doing here?'

Rendezvous with the Ravishing Rapier

6 p.m.

'NISHA TALWAR?'

'*Register mein enter kar dijiye,*' he said with a little more respect.

These security guards have a highly trained eye to sieve out sales representatives who try to use the name of some hotshot who works in the building as a passkey. I must appear to be a '*saphistikated Babu*' to him.

I filled up the idiotic registry.

Name. Address. Purpose – Murder/theft etc. Time in – five minutes later. Time out – Fill it later.

'*Wahan se andar chale jayiye* and first floor,' he said, pointing towards the entry gate to the building as if I had plans to scale the height of the building and break in from the roof.

I walked towards the gate. There was not much activity around the building. I could only make out a truck standing at the back of the building.

The building was covered entirely in thick layers of soot, dust and dirt. I followed the way indicated by the security guard and found a passageway connected to a staircase made with steps of stone and a wood railing, obviously covered in dust. I was careful not to get dust tattoos on my shirt as I went up.

The door to the floor was a contrast to the building. It promised some surprise in the offing.

As I pushed the dark brown melamine and Bakelite-coated heavy wooden door, a whiff of minty lemony sickeningly refreshing cool air hit me. The cool part of it was refreshing and the scent was nauseating.

As my eyes adjusted to the brightness of the halogen-lit office space with naked CFL bulbs that were dangling from the ceiling, I could appreciate shockingly bright-coloured graffiti style design on layered walls showing bare bricks uncoated with paint.

The office had now started interacting with the snotty me, saying, 'Who's your daddy now?'

I felt an irrepressible and involuntary shiver on my neck. Deep breaths helped me locate the reception desk.

'Hi. Welcome to Svelte.' She made it sound sassy.

'Hi. I am here to meet Nisha Talwar. I am from ...' I had totally forgotten where I was from. A few seconds of awkward silence passed....

'Cairn & Company. Yes, she is expecting you. Take a seat, please.'

It took me thirty seconds to figure out two things. One, people usually forgot their whereabouts and lost sense of the present when they saw her and the office. This was commonplace. Second, the company folder I was carrying helped her fill in the otherwise blank 'err' for me.

The next thirty seconds were spent on imagining what their coffer would look like. It would be a massive safe, of the size of a swimming pool, and Nisha Talwar would take a dip in the typical Uncle Scrooge fashion.

'Nisha will have you now, Aniket.' I did not think I heard her right. I was a half-consultant, not a pimp.

My first instinct was to say, 'No! I don't think so!'

'Excuse me?'

'Nisha. She will see you now. Go straight past that glass door. Take a right from the end of the trail and then follow it directly to her office.'

She walked back to her desk after giving me this information. Talk about performing a duty to the letter.

I opened the glass door to a flurry of activity. There wasn't much work force. Just about twenty-odd people were sitting at their respective cubicles, but they were as busy as tiny worker ants. I reached the end of the path. Before turning right, I looked to the left. There was a false wall hiding something noisy. A little peek revealed a stream of tailors manufacturing high quality goods exported worldwide. The rabbit hole was interesting as hell. It was about to get better with the meeting with the queen.

I reached the door. To my surprise, it had a coat of leather. It was a decorative, stylish veil.

The leather door confused me too. There was no way anyone could knock on a leather door.

I opened the door and peeked in and found a pair of eyes looking at me through a pair of bifocal spectacles made out of thin black sheet.

'May I ...'

'Please come in.'

I went in. There was a large tinted glass window behind her chair. Through it, I could see her private garden. Nothing could be seen leading to that garden or balcony, no visible staircase, doorway, flight of steps, etc.; yet another mystery.

The office was one of a kind. The chandelier that hung from the ceiling was throwing bright light that was absorbed by the dark wooden panels covering the walls and the wooden flooring below. Even the tabletop was a hard, smooth and dark slab of granite with dark green patterns. There was no reflective surface in the room. The only chance of a reflection was the tinted glass window that would turn into a mirror once the twilight took over. However, I was sure that there would be very bright lights in the balcony to make the small green haven still visible from the office. I had a feeling that this person was perhaps, not the happiest with herself.

She got up from her high-back leather sofa of a chair that actually could have put a majestic throne to shame. A hand was shot out at me. I took it and shook it. The grip was rather firm.

'Nisha.'

'Aniket. Pleased to meet you.'

'Likewise. Please have a seat.' The way she said it gave the impression that the seat would be hurled at me. I waited for that for a few seconds and finally sat down.

The leather chair was insanely comfortable. It was like a pre-facial massage for the butt and I instantly felt drowsy.

'What would you like to have?' She did not wait for a response and buzzed someone to get two cups of coffee.

Her impatience with my non-response was not partially her intolerance of delay. Rather, it was due to the fact that I was dumbfounded a time too many in the day right there in her office, gazing at her blazing face that had the hint of a slight pink, like the colour found on strawberry mousse and I could vouch for at least two similarities between a strawberry mousse and her.

Her face had a very angular shape, carved out of sandstone by present-day laser cutters at some hi-tech freak of an artist's workshop. The glasses she wore gave her an air of intellectual pursuit and her eyebrows curved curiously, arching above the rim of the spectacles giving her a certain diabolical demeanour. She had taken great care to look her age while her actual countenance was totally opposed to the idea.

Coming back to the purpose of the visit, I took out the questionnaire from my folder and handed it over to her just managing a few words.

'These are for the details that we require to start working on the project.'

'Hmm.' She merely glanced at them bemusedly and called for someone to join us.

For five minutes, we waited in silence as I saw her read some interesting bit of paper. She kept glancing there and back between the paper and the Mac display.

'I actually know what I have to do with the business. This is just to show some stakeholders that I have done my homework. I will e-mail your boss the contents of the report I want from your company as soon as our company's Internet connection gets fixed. I want you to advise exactly the things I want you to advise.' She said it without having to look at me. The silence must have prompted her to say that.

But, now I knew another facet of a consulting job. We were the signatories to certain CEOs' whims among other things. And this was even safer than a Chartered Accountant's audit as there was nobody governing or checking our malpractice.

'Come in.' My senses told me that no kind of 'heads up' of any sort had been given to ask for permission. The next second, two people entered the room. One carried a tray with two cups of coffee and the second looked young, like an enthusiastic employee on hire.

'Amay, this is Aniket. The consultant from Cairn. Here is the questionnaire. Please juggle the management jargon.'

He smiled and bowed his head to me, took the papers and stood there giving them a scan.

'With all due respect, madam ...'

'Nisha, please.'

'With all due respect, Nisha, it is not just jugglery. These are important things that help us give our clients the deliverables.' I was uneasy with the way this businessperson was talking about management fundas.

She smiled. Amay also smiled. Even the coffee guy smiled. Everybody apparently knew something except for me. Although, the coffee guy had just been smiling to follow suit.

She took a sip of the coffee and dismissed both of them, asking Amay to get the papers back to the office in fifteen minutes.

'Aniket, I'm sure that you have heard this from a great number of people that there is a lot of difference between what you have studied in your business school and what actually happens. It's true. The fundas you have read are applied by everyone without the need of calling them something. People who do that can apply them easily. People who first learn the fundas become their slaves and have a hard time looking for that jugglery even in the simplest of management equations.'

I felt quite taken aback at this blatant disregard of established management fundas.

'Well, I suppose jugglery would definitely help if picked up by certain people and applied to perfection. The thing or phenomena that you describe, which implies sub-conscious application of fundas is, in my opinion, for a non-learned person, left to the mercy of probability a little too much. Having understood theory and its application actually saves time.'

'Touché. But, as of now, the percentage of successful people divided into the two categories we have discussed would favour my odds.'

I was beginning to truly enjoy the conversation, blasphemous as the discussion was to the idea of management education, it was certainly esoteric.

'I don't think so. What about Indra Nooyi, Ratan Tata, K M Birla, Ambani brothers – all of whom have received management education.'

'Oh, please. For one, most of them had business grooming from their childhood and others have been plain brilliant with an IQ level that promised them some great deeds in the world.'

'IQ isn't everything when it comes to greatness.'

'Tch. I think we can continue with this sometime later. Suffice to tell you that Indian MBAs are actually just full of technical words without the skills of negotiation. Amay is from some B-school in some godforsaken NCR area, he takes twenty grand a month and creates corporate communication for me with all the word jumbles.' This time, her smile accompanied a raised eyebrow.

'Whatever will happen to this country?'

I picked up the cup of coffee to take a sip when she said, 'Don't drink that. The coffee is crap. I usually offer it to people I do not give a damn about.' She had pretended to take a sip from her cup after all.

'You gladly accepted coffee from a client. You must be new to this? Are you?' she asked rhetorically.

'It is my first day at work.' I pleaded naivety and the innocence in my tone was an attempt to escape without incidence.

'Oh dear. That figures.' She was laughing. 'It is perfectly okay to have coffee at a client's by the way. I was just messing with you.' Her evil grin was almost hair-raising.

'I think I should make up for that. Do you like whiskey?' She got up from her throne and walked towards a cabinet in the corner of the room. There was a painting of a drunken lady on the wall next to the cabinet. She tugged at a handle protruding from the cabinet and the cabinet doors gave way to a tray that slid out with a few exquisite crystal bottles filled with liquor.

She was wearing an ethnic-styled long black skirt, high enough to show a fairy tattoo on her ankle and a tattoo made in the shape of an anklet that wound round her ankle. And the stilettos she wore had daggers for heels.

'No thanks. I don't think drinking at work is a good idea.'

'Why? It is already after office hours. You don't get paid for time beyond 6 p.m. now, do you?'

'Err ... no. But still. I have to get back to the office.'

She hadn't cared to listen to my reply anymore than to humour a rhino in her little garden.

'Consultants ... you bill by the lunch morsels, by the taxi rides, by the copier pages and comprehensively, by the hour. You are charging me thirty freaking grand per hour. Did you know that? How much are you getting paid? Enough perks?'

I just gave her an indignant stare. It didn't bother her. Ever seen a fly bother a tigress?

'Sad.' She poured herself a large measure from one of the bottles.

She took a large sip and gulped down the spirit. 'Suit yourself.' She tilted her head to one side and started walking towards me.

There was no escape and there was no saying what this ferocious lady was capable of.

She came and leaned her back against the table, next to where I was seated.

'This is a big bad world, Aniket. You are a sweet guy. How do you hope to survive? Don't follow orders that your heart does not give you permission to. And this is not an oxymoron.'

She poked my nose with her forefinger and took another large sip.

I thought it best to hear it over without chartering any consolation, condolences, advice, rude 'shut ups', although shouting out a loud 'shut up' was very tempting indeed.

'My husband is an MBA from some great college that the pink newspapers just won't shut up about. And, perverse to what your common rationality would have you believe, he is the biggest swine I know. I sincerely hope that you are saved from the kind of transformation the corporate world can have on you. I will tell you a little story, Aniket. It is just for your ears. Don't tell it to anyone else, okay?'

I was trying to recall where I had put my 'instant shrink' magic potion. I wanted to shrink right there in my seat and get the heck out of this place.

'I was leading a perfectly happy life when two shocks that I gave to my husband ruined everything.'

I looked at a large framed photograph of two children on the wall opposite to the drunken woman portrait wall to avoid looking at her.

'The first shock was when my father gave me this business, whatever was still left of it before he passed away. My husband must have expected to be the rightful owner of ... well ... mine ... and his and almost all inheritances from the entire fatherhood of the world. Somehow, blended Scotch whiskey helped him get over it. The second shock that finally unshackled the beast was when I turned around this business into what it is today. He could possibly not digest the fact that my profits from this place were twice his annual salary. Obviously, the equations surrounding the importance of time for us as individuals were too much for him to handle. And so, ...'

She rambled on for some time about some children, boarding schools, alimony, etc. Then suddenly her hand was on my cheeks as I sat paralysed in my chair. Correction, her hand with perfectly manicured, blade like, shiny nails had grabbed hold of my lower jaw in a soft but firm embrace. She held my gaze and just sat there peering.

Maybe, she was just doing some power yoga meditation pose for which one requires a partner. But I failed to see any meditative benefit in it for me. I was hoping for it to have some 'sedative' benefit in it for her.

I did not know whether it was my imagination or was she really getting closer.

I was frozen into disbelief by her violation of a fellow citizen's comfort zone. Nonetheless, I sat there frozen, very still. My strategy could be described as 'playing dead'. I was trying to recall some Discovery channel show in which 'lady cougars' were hopefully shown to discard dead animals. I could recall no such thing. So I started praying that she would have seen some such show and would know better than to prey on a smaller, dead animal.

As an answer to my prayers, in the next instant, she just let my face go, stood up and sat back on her throne.

Seconds that almost certainly felt like hours later, Amay walked in with the questionnaire filled up.

'Done with it, Nisha. Take a look.'

In a brisk movement of her slender looking, and what I now knew for sure, weight-trained hand, she took the papers from him and handed them to me without the slightest botheration.

'I will see you around, Aniket. Please escort him to the gate, Amay.'

'Goodbye', I croaked and good riddance, I hoped.

Amay led me out the modest labyrinthine of that wonderland. I had forgotten the simple L route back.

As we walked to the main entry door to the floor, Amay looked at me to bid au revoir but said something else entirely judging by the fact of what was written all over my face. I was feeling a little perturbed and disturbed at the atrocious nature of the world.

'Did she tell you the story about a divorced husband? She does that a lot. Don't mind it. Take care man. See you.' He mocked an informal salute.

I walked out of the building completely dazed. Sometimes, the God Almighty makes one the witness of unusual events, the rationale of which is completely unfathomable.

I could do nothing about what had transpired or what was threatening to transpire. How would a boss take such a complaint from a new employee about a client? What would this kind of thing come under, harassment or adam-teasing (If something like this existed)? None. What did that woman really want? What was she going for? With full knowledge that anyone from her staff could barge in at any moment!

And why on Earth was I thinking about a divorced, sassy, pretty, alcoholic mother of two who tried to land a smacker on me just for being argumentative? Now that was unfair.

Too much wonderland is bad for health. I wanted to put as much distance between me and that place as possible. I found the cab parked nearby, jumped in and got the driver to waste another one of his *beedis*. This bank was ready to '*loot*' the robbers. '*Jaldi chalo. Jaldi.*' (Let us get the heck out of here.)

Highway to Hell

6.45 p.m.

'WHY DON'T YOU MOVE THIS DAMN CAR?' SOMEBODY SHOUTED.

I kept looking ahead, staring at the big bleary red eye of the thin yellow colour monster. I wanted to stare it down into turning green. Humming a song by Fuzon and minding my own business, I noticed the high-pitched sound of giggling that had travelled through two glass windows and carried over two buzzing engines.

I could not help but investigate the source. I looked to my right and straight at one of the forms of PDA (public display of affection). The two creatures were in a love duel, cuddling and canoodling each other and snatching at some mobile phone as an excuse to keep the romance thematic and purposeful to the untrained eye. It was an adorable scene because of the morally correct and ethically platonic thinking of my brain. I just laughed patronisingly and smirked to myself.

Alas! The girl brat sitting in the non-driver seat saw my reaction to their supposedly hush-hush moment. Then, the human defence mechanism kicked in. She began to stare at me. A wide Cheshire cat mocking smile followed the stare. Then, she laughed heartily and her boyfriend joined in. He was still holding her and trying to communicate the point, 'I am in my dad's gift with my dad's friend's wife's gift to me. I don't care whether you noticed or not.' I smiled and looked away ahead saying, 'Point taken.' So, these culprits are the ones that mate, generate off-springs with two helpings of beauty and half a helping of brain.

The lights turned green. The guy turned off the car lights so that the film-coated glass would turn opaque again. They drove off first, showing off the pickup of the BMW against my chug-a-lot cab. Well, money may not be everything after all; it is the only thing.

'*Main bhi BMW chalaya karta tha.*'

'*Kya keh rahe hain?*'

'Yes, sahib. I used to be driver of a very wealthy seth. They gave me much lower pay than what I earn driving this car. That job was about pride, respect and comfort.'

'But then, why did you leave that job?'

'Risk.'

'What kind of risk?'

'I was paid .01% per month of what the car was worth. In addition to that, if something at all were to happen to the car, my pay got deducted till the cost of damage got recovered.'

'But did something like that ever happen?'

'Unfortunately, yes. Rear view mirror was stolen when the car was under my supervision. It was worth 50,000.'

'But what about car insurance?'

'Rich people don't take the trouble of paper work, sahib. Insurance is for big things like when the car gets damaged in an accident.'

The notorious knack of high-end luxury cars in Delhi to run over people and hit motorcyclists was part of folklore and the professional codebook of drivers.

'Yes. That is when they really get to use insurance money and additional investment in bribes, etc.'

'Sahib, it is dirtier and murkier than you think. But as to why I drive this cab? It is true that it gives me body pain, but it is relatively, if only marginally, more money and less risk of life.'

When was the last time I met someone who did not have any problems in life? Gladly, never. Otherwise, somebody would give that person a problem eventually.

At length, persevering through the traffic, I reached the office.

A Hard Day's Night

7 p.m.

All I wanted at that point in time was to grab my bag and scram.

I got into the lift. I was the only one in it. I deserved nothing less than not having to meet anyone anymore for the day. I had had enough.

The phone rang. It was Girish.

'Hello.'

'Hi Aniket. Have you reached the office yet?' The hypocrite was already on his way home. I could hear the growls, roars and scowls of the wild traffic in the background.

'Yes.'

'Did you collect the information?' Yes, more than you can ever imagine, you moron.

'Yes.'

'Where are you right now?'

'I'm going up to my cubicle to get my bag.' That was another very wrong answer.

'Well, do something for me. We need to start working on this project tomorrow morning as a priority. Please type in this information in the 'Risk Scanner' and the 'ClienServe' software. You will find the shortcuts to these programs on the desktop of Shivangi's computer. Call me from the office phone when you get there.'

He disconnected without giving me any opportunity whatsoever to explain my case.

I shouted out certain expletives, kicked the lift from the inside but soon realised that a lift at more than 50 feet height hanging over nothing but air does not take any kind of aggression lightly. The lift opened at the eighth floor and I dragged my feet to the cubicle.

The office seemed deserted. Perhaps, some epidemic had run amok engulfing every soul in my department. One either feels happy to be in office till late hours or feels very frustrated. Happy because you can do whatever on God's fanciest creation on Earth and nobody would be there to tell you off. Your civility is the only thing standing in the way of your going overboard and taking a leak on your boss' chair rather than just sitting on it. It is immense power. Immense frustration, on the other hand, is the result of the relative view of things coupled with jealousy or the cancellation of an extremely important date when you had the chance to get laid or something as important as that to other people as that date would be to a bachelor, respectively.

The cross-border department still had a few people working on something or the other. They did not look as enthusiastic or happy about their work as they had been looking in the morning. Why would they be happy? Some had missed their evening workout, some would be denied their workout in the night, some who didn't have a chance in the world for any workout whatsoever would have to contend with a late, cold, maybe microwave-heated, dry dinner. Only a few were actually glad that they did not have to go back home till late; and just use their own homes as bed-and-breakfast joints. And then there were those like me, who were undecided on the category of late office workers that they would fall in.

Large parts of where my department was were dark. The lights had been switched off. This made the outside view prominently visible.

I could see the MG Road winding like a yellow python, leading back to Delhi, to home, to comfort and respite from this terrible and indispensible world. The cars were moving in queues trying to get the heck out of the concrete jungle of Gurgaon and were forced to play Tetris or the 'brick game' at every roadblock and bottle neck. Bike riders were particularly adept at playing this game. They would weave around the traffic until they scratched and scathed other cars on their way towards the cause of the halted traffic making the situation more complex and vicious. The only difference between the brick game and the traffic was that the brick game allowed the rows of bricks to disappear, while in this case, they just piled on haphazardly to make some hideous modern art piece.

I went to the edge of the floor where there was just a glass pane separating me and a 70-foot drop and admired the beauty and the ugliness of the night time view of the corporate city. It was a picture-perfect moment for a hero gazing across the city skyline, standing at a towering height and having brazen thoughts exuding the hope of sanity to the insane and the phobic masses looking up at him. It was a great anti-climax from a movie where the hero has conquered the world and now watches over it, as if it belongs to him, awaiting any cry for help. The hero, the saviour of the world, rescuing damsels in distress and....

Now, I knew why this world was Greek to me. Megalomania came easily to the most unsuspecting autocrats and lords reining over bits and parts of this world.

My cellphone's loud ringtone snapped me out of some obtuse brain activity for which only corporate ennui is to blame.

It was Girish, again, the demigod of mundane work and the harbinger of destruction of personal life. I had to grudgingly, reluctantly, save his number to the phonebook so that, in the future, I could choose not to take his call whenever he called on some holiday. Or whenever he would call to call me back upstairs while I am all set and ready to leave the office, or call to give instructions in trickles due to his own ageing, failing memory, or above all, when he calls me right after the official semi-annual review to give me the real performance review.

'Hi. I was just booting the comp ... I'll call you back in five minutes.' The lies and the liberty given by phone calls are such a boon.

I think I only imagined him replying an 'okay'. He could put any Scrooge to shame. Or maybe that is how managers increased their cool quotient, by being brief and strictly to the point. And that totally explains why some brief encounters in the lobby and supposed moments of peace in the washroom are full of guffawing laughter on raunchy jokes and piteous laughs on sad but still bawdy anecdotes.

Finally, I began walking with a grimace towards the desk to start with the donkey work. I was smirking when I sat on the chair. Actually, midway, I had taken a stop at my boss's cubicle and had sat in his chair and saw what he saw day in and out. There was a calendar pinned to the board covering the cubicle walls. There were many reminder notes on post-its pasted all over the desk. Some of them were very interesting. Cryptic and interesting, written in scrawny handwriting, the notes were too tempting to not charter a guess into their meaning. There was a calendar too with funny markings. A number was placed besides the hand-drawn symbol of a cradle on the date of 14th May. I explored the rest of the calendar.

After spending five minutes there, I found out that he had three small kids aged three, two and one. Somebody had been keeping the Mrs busy. He had three girls. It was a wonder that in an age when the cases of female foeticide and cost of raising a child were both rising high and fast, this guy was doing his bit for the womanhood of India; increasing their count. I would not really like to think of any obvious ulterior or even nefarious motives and reasons bearing the stamp of social sanctions responsible for such a hat trick.

The mobile buzzed wildly in my pocket again and I slid towards the workstation. I put the phone on silent as it flashed the boss' name. It finally gave up after a few seconds. Then the orchestra picked up again. Only after switching the laptop on and logging in did I pick the phone with the excuse of having been to the washroom ready with me.

'Yeah Girish. The comp. is on now. Tell me.'

He gave me the instructions without any extra word and I was to follow it to the letter. Maybe he thought that any extra word would translate into me doing something that was not asked for; as if he might let slip the truth about what he thinks that kids my age should do on the evening of their first day at work, go celebrate with friends at a party.

Anyways, I started with the data entry. It was boring as hell. It took me twenty minutes to do the damn thing. Even more irksome was the fact that that could obviously have been done even in the morning.

I was so engrossed in getting through with the grotesque task, that I did not notice an icon bobbling on the icon tray. It was Outlook messenger indicating that there were unread mails in my inbox. I opened Shivangi's inbox.

The last e-mail was from HR. But surprisingly, it showed the time as 6 p.m. And even more shocking was the subject of the e-mail, 'Pickup arranged for hospital'.

'Dear Team,
As you are all aware that our very own, Shivangi met with an accident today in the afternoon after she had gotten off from the half-day; we have arranged cabs for any of you who wish to go and visit her at the hospital and offer condolences and solace to herself and her family. Please assemble at the main gate area at 6.45 p.m.
Thanks,
Smriti Kapoor
HR Manager'

Was it the height of crude and numb cruelty or just a brainless act from a complete nincompoop to send this e-mail as a group mail so that it reaches Shivangi's inbox as well?

I just couldn't stop myself from reading certain other e-mails. The mail just below the one from HR had no subject. I opened it. It said, 'Sorry,' and nothing else. Spooky. The sender was some tssharma with a non-corporate id from a free for all e-mail service.

There was no e-mail in the entire month that spoke anything about her being fired.

The phone buzzed wildly and rather too loudly. Or perhaps I was just caught by my phone in an unethical act of reading an injured and broken colleague's e-mail, which was weighing on my conscious and that had made the ear drums more sensitive!

'Yes, Girish. The work is done.'

'Thanks. See you tomorrow.'

He was already home. There was no sound of traffic in the background anymore; he was back in the comfort of his household where he ruled over three kids and a wife who lived in the constant fear of all kinds of labour; of household chores, love and procreation.

I felt a rumbling somewhere inside my head followed by one in my stomach. I was hungry, drained of energy and longing for the sweet warmth and comfort of my home. It was time to go home after a long first day of work.

I picked up and packed my stuff, slung the backpack on my shoulder and made my way to the lobby.

I kicked the door of the lift after having pressed the call button several times and waiting for five minutes for the lift only to realise that the lift had been shut down. Some noble soul came flying to the lobby and stated the obvious to my utter annoyance, 'the lift has been closed down.' Yes, I think I figured that much out myself.

'The lift is in operation only till 7.30 p.m. Take the stairs.'
Oh really, I was all game to go base-jumping to take revenge on all my bones.

He went down the staircase like grease lightening. Some people do get excited at the prospect of finishing a long day's work and taking the staircase down eight flights; on their way to premature knee damage.

I trudged carefully and started my slow descent down, 'the rabbit hole'.

The setting seemed to have heard my comment and reverberated back as the heart-rending sobs of a girl.

Poor thing! Perhaps she couldn't read the warning signs strewn across the whole damn office setup. There were little hints hidden in codes waiting to be deciphered. E.g. Re-arrange the letters of the word 'Employee' and you get a hint of your post-joining behaviour, 'Me *Yelp* Oe!' or a hint of what other people are supposed to do to an employee, 'Peel Me Yo!' in which case, you coolly invite people to peel you only because you are an employee! Or consider the word BOSS – the anagram gives SOBS depending on your level of piss-off.

I was on the final few steps making my way to the ground floor exit when I was drawn further down the stairs on the way to the level 1 parking. The faint sobs had carried me down, right to the parking lot.

Damsel in Distress

8 p.m.

She was sitting there, with her head in her hands and heart in the pit of her stomach. Her long hair was all over the place. It wasn't her clothes. It wasn't her voice. It wasn't until I was next to her, touched her shoulder, said, 'hey there,' that I looked at her face. I shouted, 'woah!' I was shocked at a scary face that had a distraught look about it and a concoction of black liner and tears smeared all over her eyes and cheeks. I realised that this was Tia.

'Hey, what happened?' My voice had never sounded more concerned!

'Please go away,' she said through her sobs, trying to wipe her cheeks clean of the smeared kajal and tears but instead smearing the mix even more evenly over her face.

'Hey. C'mon. I am here to help. Whatever it is. Tell me.'

'You really don't need to hear this. You have just joined. I don't think it's good for you...'

'Tia, I know you better than that and you know me better than that. Out with it now!' Being firm with her sort of did it and she gave in, pouring out whatever had transpired.

She had overheard two morons in the office gossiping about her. They called her the 'loneliest person in office' and gossiped about her alleged affair that had taken place with someone in the office. It was one thing after another. Before that, the boss had given her some honest feedback on her performance which was very forthcoming on the 'didn't do' and 'can't do' aspects. She had already cryptically told me how the office had taken someone important out of her daily life. This breakdown was on the cards.

But what happened after she poured her heart out was equally unimaginable.

I said to her: 'These people are like that only. You just concentrate on what you can do. Just quit this place. Get a change of pace and base. You know, there was this colleague of mine who sat right behind me. In the morning, she was hale and hearty, and all of a sudden, she was told that she was going to get a pink slip from the office. She started crying and left, much to my embarrassment. And now, when I was working at her computer, I saw a mail from the HR informing everybody in the department that she had met with an accident and cabs have been arranged for everybody to go and see her in the hospital. But I think something more devious happened.... I am not sure but I think she tried to commit...'

The problem was that I was looking straight ahead and not at her face while she was blurting out the longest lasting emotional fountain trigger known to humankind. While I was thoughtlessly barfing out the ingredients for her next soup, her face had gone from solemn to sullen to scandalised. Had I looked at her face, I would have known that it was time to stop. But sadly, that didn't happen.

What did happen was Tia breaking loose from my arm around her shoulder with so much force that her elbow knocked my nose. Cursing out in pain and blinded by tears, I watched a blur run up the staircase out of sight. I stood up shakily and also ran up the stairs, blindly trusting my legs that were used to climb stairs to my own son-of-a-Qutab Minar-fourth storey flat in West Delhi.

I reached the ground floor landing and watched a blur of long hair and white stilettos rush towards the fire exit. I followed. And presto! There was no one there.

The click of the service lift doors closing made me turn around to see the lift control display show an arrow pointing upward. I ran up the staircase that wound around the lift shaft.

Huffing, panting, halting at each landing to check whether the lift regurgitated the occupant and then re-starting with persistent vigour made my head go light and breathing out of sync with a madly beating heart.

Amidst the unwanted excitement, my phone rang again. It was my soon-to-be-ex-girlfriend. And against my finer instincts, I picked up the phone.

'Hey.'

'How was your day? Where are you?'

'Umm ... I am in office.'

'Why are you still in office? Why are they working you late on your first day? What is all that noise; you joined a services company right? And why do you sound out of breath and running?'

'I'm in the middle of something very important and time-consuming!' I tried to make it sound as important as it was.

'Are you saying that to avoid me?' Bah! Girls!

'No dear. It is very important.' No wonder she was soon to be my ex-girlfriend. She was giving me all the reasons right there, in the middle of a life-saving trekking adventure.

'Is it?' asked she in a sarcastic, sceptic tone.

'Trust me. It is a matter of life and death.' Reached floor 5. 'I will call you in some time. Bye.' I hung up the phone. But then it rang again!

'Hi, Ma.'

'Late to be home on the first day at work. What kind of heartless and cruel people are they?'

'Well, I seem to have hit the ground running, Ma. I have to get some documents prepared and have to do some running around for that. I will call back in five minutes. Too busy. Got to go.'

Reached sixth floor.

I hung up and concentrated on making my way to Her Psychotic Sexiness who had decided to jump to glory.

The least worst thing that could happen was her leap of faith to the ground floor, from whatever floor she had decided to go cliff diving from, without the parachute which would kill her if she was lucky and paralyse her, if she wasn't. And the worst part would be the whole mess being partly my fault.

In all my chasing, running 'Wile E Coyote' glory to, yes, very ironically, save the 'Roadrunner'; the climax was extremely ominous.

'TIA!' I remember the shout. I had never in my life shouted as loudly as I had to, to stop that girl.

Then it all happened in five split seconds that seemed to stretch to an eternity. The overhead bulb on what, to my recollection, was the 7th floor, blinked at the shift of energy source from the generator to the power grid, I saw her limply crashing into the railing on the floor, and grabbed her by the waist as her body leaned over the caressing comfort of the cool evening air.

Her momentum dragged my body over the railing as well, with her waist and mine acting like one of those SUVs from a thriller movie that drags halfway over the edge and waits for a bird to sit on its hanging bonnet. I somehow stretched my right leg and tried to put in more weight to the safer side. And luckily, I succeeded. Yet unluckily, my foot missed the top landing and slipped to the lower floor.

Off balance, with Tia still filling my arms, I fell back as my head hit the wall behind me and just before everything went dark, I felt the back of Tia's head butt my forehead and nose as my head ricocheted from the wall again.

In Two Shakes of a Lamb's Tale

8.37 p.m.

I opened my eyes to one of the floors. Somebody had turned on very bright lights with no sympathies whatsoever for my corneas.

'Hey. How do you feel?'

Guess, who gets the top honours for asking a ruddy stupid, moronically obvious and clichéd question?

'Splendid.' Stupendous.

'Sorry for all that. You got knocked out. I think you hit your head on the wall. Then ... I got you here somehow.'

As the consciousness flowed through the rest of my body sending back signals to my brain, the skin on my back felt strangely sore and throbbing, aping the reaction of my head. I examined whatever of my shirt I could see. She had used me as a floor mop in her grand effort to get me here. I was angry now.

'What do you mean sorry? What kind of person just runs off to the top of a building to jump off it? We could have been dead right now! Do you even understand what that means? Have you totally lost it? Tell me whatever is happening here right now!'

I was bellowing at her at the top of my lungs. She timidly picked up a glass of water from a nearby table and handed it to me. I took it, drank the water and waited for her to start.

'Well ... I was in a relationship with ... it is just that I never expected that she would try to commit ... but it all became too much ...' and then she broke down with typhoons of gigantic tears washing her cheeks.

'She blamed me! As if I was the reason for all that was happening to her ... her work performance, snide comments by colleagues ... all of it!'

'Hey ... hey ... hey ... Shhh! Quiet now. I do understand. Seems like you have been in the rough for quite some time now. It does take a toll on the best of us.' Moreover, it is so especially when somebody is 'experimenting'. At least, it was a consolation to deduce which of the two was the man in the 'relationship' with all the blaming and pseudo-focus on work.

'And that ass, perverted, loser, divorced, balding, frustrated scumbag of a senior always ogling at females says that I am the loneliest person he has ever met!' she ranted.

I was quiet, staring at her face in mocking disbelief. She broke down again and told me the rest through her sobs, 'I heard him discussing sleaze with his equally sad friend.' Pause. 'I am strong. I won't quit. Reporting him will not get him fired. He has been reported five times and his only penalty was a cancelled promotion. Somehow, I will get him for this.' Her tears dried up with the end of the statement and I could see a steely resolve instead.

I just talked and listened to her and used all the appeasing, calming expressions I had ever come across.

'Hey. The janitors take over at around this time. We should get moving. I've already ordered a taxi for you to go home.'

'What about you?'

'You go. I just want to be alone.'

What a self-righteous, self-destructive fool.

'Okay, listen young lady. You have no hope in heaven that I am going to leave you alone after all this. What kind of a dumb ass do you take me to be?'

She just looked at me.

'Wait! Don't you answer that! I am no dumb ass.' I winked at her. That did make her laugh and gave me relief.

'Come. Let's go. We'll go get a nice dinner.'

'Umm ... I am not hungry.'

'Well, you can watch me eat. You should know that people have offered to pay me or just pay for the dinner for watching me eat. It's a real privilege.' Another hearty laugh followed. Her appetite would be back by the time we would reach the restaurant.

We climbed down the staircase and reached the taxi. We both sat together on the back seat.

'Take us to Khan Market, Sardarji,' instructed she as we sat. It was good to see her taking an initiative towards normalcy.

We stopped talking after ten minutes of the car ride and I was back looking at the outside view trying to distract myself. The incomplete metro-line construction looked ghoulish against the night sky. There were also some half-demolished buildings from the ceiling drive in Delhi.

After a while, she rested her body against my chest and let her head fall back on my shoulder.

I started humming, rather, crooning a soothing song to fit the moment.

Some things had been waiting to shout peek-a-boo at this little romantic moment. Sardarji turned on the music system of the car and the volume was high by default.

'*O Veera chukk de Bullutt, puttrol hai menga!*' (Hey dude, sell off your big bike 'cause petrol is expensive). Plus ... speed breaker! Damn, my chest was caught unaware and my breath was somewhat knocked out of me spoiling what otherwise would have been a perfectly romantic moment.

'Go slow, Sardarji. And please change the music,' I told the driver. He looked into the rearview mirror, bared his huge white chicken munching teeth and said, 'Yes, sir!' He then put the radio on to a station that played the cheesiest Bollywood numbers on earth at a barely audible volume. I tried to concentrate on my breathing just for the heck of it.

We went past the mandir of a great sage and saint on our way. It got me thinking how the most frugal of all saints ever to walk the earth would feel if he finds out how much money people donate for the upkeep of a shrine erected in his name. The most noticeable of the 'followers' were white-collar folk. They talk about religion and belief as something alien in their conference rooms and here they are seen trying to bribe their way into the next promotion and even promoting alms outside the complex.

Anyhow, I bowed towards the saint's idol after catching a glimpse of it from the outside and asked him for his blessings for the girl right next to me. *That* did not cost a thing.

I suddenly became aware of how close she was to me. I noticed that I was breathing in harmony with her expanding ribcage. In that moment, with help from a strong urge spurred by my selfish streak, I sent my hopes to heaven for even the slimmest possibility that she could still swing my way.

'Would you like to go watch a play on Sunday? They are playing *Halfway House*, an adaptation of *Aadhe Adhure* in English. It was written by Mohan Rakesh.'

'Sure. I would love to. What is it about?'

'It is a story about an unfulfilled life ... life's inevitable continuity....'

I had no damn clue what the play was about.

We were drained and feeling drowsy. I thought we might have even taken a good 15-minute nap before a jackass trying out his 4x4's big horns woke us up. She yawned and grinned at me.

'I know what you are thinking.' I was in a mood for mischief.

'Oh, yeah? Like what?'

'Well, we just gave a whole new meaning to the expression, 'sleeping together'.' Her mouth gaped, half-smiling in surprise and she threw that wide-eyed look into my face.

'What the hell? I can't believe you said ...!' She heeled my toe and punched my shoulder. It did not hurt.

'Oww. Cut it out!'

'That serves you right!'

'Oh c'mon. You are still laughing. It was funny. Admit it! I know a funny quip when I deliver one.' Noting this reaction, I retained the quip's successor which was something about the norm that 'getting physical' generally comes before the 'sleeping together' bit.

'You're an idiot!' She said. I took out the chocolate in my pocket and handed it over to her. She took it. She smiled. 'A cute one at that,' she added. I smiled.

Still, Let's Call it a Day!

9.01 p.m.

'YOU KNOW I'D REALLY LIKE A FEW TEQUILA SHOTS RIGHT NOW.'

I peeked into her eyes waiting for her to start laughing. She did not laugh.

'Are you serious?' I had to ask.

She laughed hard and long. Even the driver looked at us through the rearview mirror.

'So you officially think of me as some freak show?'

I was flushed. I shook my head.

'Just a little bit weird maybe. You really need to put in some effort though. You've just met me dear and frankly, you ain't seen nothin' yet!' I beamed at her.

'You've changed, Ani. A lot. And for the better.' Look who's talking.

'Let's see what you have to say after those tequila shots.' I winked at her. She elbowed my rib lightly.

The car pulled into Khan market.

I wondered what the second day at work would be like.

Epilogue

Off-site Shocks

Vodka was certainly not my thing. I was glad that it wasn't on offer. Nonetheless, there were quite a few whisky and Scotch brands available which are consumed for their price and brand name rather than the taste. Proof of the pie may be in eating but the respect for a drink, for these connoisseurs was in its smoothness, which is the only adjective that they know apart from 'slosh-ability', which could be discerned from their drink etiquette, or the absence of it.

Maybe this was another one of those awfully exciting team-building exercises initiated by the HR function.

'Here! Have a drink, dear boy,' said the senior manager, Girish, handing a highball glass filled with a large serving of Scotch whisky, soda and ice. I did not hesitate to take the drink from him. His eyes were menacing, glistening and drunk, bloodshot red.

'Everyone!' he addressed the India team (at the bar) out loud, 'this is Aniket and he has been with us for a month now. He is a really bright boy.' Damn right, I am bright. These guys had been working me on Saturdays and extracting some inhuman measure of work. This appreciation was for his own good.

Everyone raised a drink to me and said, 'welcome.' The after-effect of alcohol made them sing out the word in unison, with a few doing the harmonies.

I raised my glass, said 'cheers!' and took a shadow sip and peeked over the crowd's shoulder for a plant I could pour the liquor in, this night. The whisky was Indian *thurra*. Although, the colour was dark gold, which was confidingly deceiving, the body was the nastiest cough syrup that unfolded itself on the palate like a yawning porcupine and a nauseating finish of egg yolk. Thus, my changed plans did not involve drinking at all. In fact, if things went as planned, I was in for intoxication through something much more potent.

Meanwhile, the cons had found their counterparts from other departments and were challenging one another to a bottoms-up. It would certainly take more than liquor to up their bottoms. At least, alcohol will make them light-headed enough to feel their bottoms set afloat. I was just glad that they were busy doing that and numbing their thick perceptive organs with spirit.

I shook innumerable hands, scowled and grinned at the faces. I made my way to a quiet green corner where I could drain my glass and do the impatient waiting, peacefully.

Alas! One of those easily envied, caprice trigger bearing drunk guys arrived probably jealous about something.

'Hi! It's good that you are standing here. People are bumping into each other so much today.' I noticed that his shirt had also had a sip of his drink.

'There would be a mass social sensitivity reporting tomorrow morning. The HR will have their hands full.'

'Well, these kinds of things don't go reported.'

'What do you mean?' I was really punished for not exercising caution here.

'Well, if someone comes and...' He nabbed the back of my neck between his bicep and arm ... 'Do this ... there is nothing to report. Other persons can just deny.' His grip was rather firm. I firmly put his hand away, keeping my calm on the drunkard's shameful act.

'I can still report this. People have told me about how convincing I can be. Let's do this experiment. What say?'

'Hey, sorry man! I was just kidding. Don't report that.'

'Even I was kidding. Excuse me!'

I excused myself from the slippery fellow and took a stone-laid path cutting across the private sand beach back to the resort rooms. The wait was already too much.

This off-site was really surreal. It was so full of fun, well, apart from the deathly morose training and sessions and some godforsaken HR exercises that were totally unbecoming of a self-appreciating and respectable individual. There was so much time to spend with Tia. And she had promised to come dressed, all guns blazing at my *'neeyat'*. But, the wait had been too long.

To reduce the waiting time or maybe to spend the waiting time, I walked back towards the porch. I noticed that a girl was sitting near a fireplace set up next to the porch. She looked beautiful. The view was hidden and with every step, some bit of the scene became clearer. My heartbeat went thump-thump-

thump-thump-skip-thump-thump-thump-thump-skip! My girl was sitting with another girl and given my girl's story of her recent past, the sweat beads on my forehead were anything but surprising. The other girl was crying.

I went over to them and smiled at Tia who smiled back dryly to reassure me of monogamy but then said, 'she was attacked … The guy who did it is…' She whispered the last part to me.

The name of the culprit did not come as a shock at all. But as I sat there with them, and listened to the whole story, I breathed to myself, 'Wow … front row tickets again!'